Double
Lives

EX LIBRIS

Double Lives

Stephen Wall

BLOOMSBURY

'The Bridge' first appeared in *Soho Square II*, 1989

First published 1991
Copyright © 1991 by Stephen Wall

The moral right of the author
has been asserted

Translation of 'Der Doppelgänger' by Heinrich Heine
(used as an epigraph), in *The Penguin Book of Lieder*
translated by S. S. Prawer (Penguin Books, 1964),
copyright © S. S. Prawer, 1964.

Bloomsbury Publishing Ltd, 2 Soho Square,
London W1V 5DE

A CIP catalogue record for this
book is available from the British
Library

ISBN 0 7475 0910 7

10 9 8 7 6 5 4 3 2 1

Typeset by Hewer Text Composition Services, Edinburgh
Printed in Great Britain by Butler and Tanner Ltd,
Frome and London

[1]

> . . . nor doth the eye itself,
> That most pure spirit of sense, behold itself,
> Not going from itself: but eye to eye opposed
> Salutes each other with each other's form;
> For speculation turns not to itself
> Till it hath travelled and is mirrored there
> Where it may see itself.

Shakespeare, *Troilus and Cressida*

A DOUBLE LIFE

The first time I saw her was among the shadows of the lower library. Because the summer light outside was so bright the bulbs behind the parchment lampshades seemed to shed no more gleam than candles would. The iron-barred windows were tall but narrow, set at regular intervals round the stone building's circumference, and the long reading tables radiated out to them like the spokes of a wheel. The ornate plaster ceiling was very high (although there was another reading room above it), so that the heavy bookcases beneath looked cowed, for all their volumes.

She was sitting at the far end of my table, by the window but turned away from it. The exterior light suffused the outer strands of her hair, making a peripheral haze round the dim impassive face. She kept very still, so intent did she appear to be on her page, but even so her image blurred a little as I covertly watched. Suddenly she closed the books in front of her, put her pen and papers in a polythene bag, and started to walk out. Her summer skirt was long and dragged on the steps up to the door; perhaps a hem had dropped. I found myself going through the pantomime of checking my watch (unreliable anyway), affecting to be amazed at the time, and packing up hastily to cover my impulse to overtake her and contrive a meeting,

5

suggest coffee, even a drink. It was a routine I'd seen others perform.

The intensity of the midday sun after the library's shade made me blink. As I got used to the light I thought I saw her retreating in the perspective between two high college walls before abruptly turning right and out of view. When I got to the same spot myself there was no sign of her. The road, recently pedestrianized, was disconcertingly empty. I went on to where it met the broad street which as usual was full of people. Most of them were locals going about their business with indigenous confidence, but some were tourists who eddied confusedly, not sure where they were going or what they ought to be looking at.

It occurred to me that she might have gone into the bookshop, but she was not in any of the departments.

*

I went out into the street, and was again surprised by the heat of the sun. It felt like being abroad — an impression intensified by the scraps of French spoken by passing visitors, although it was too early in the season for there to be many of them.

I turned into the market in quest of cooler air, still hoping for a chance glimpse of her. It was a covered area with parallel alleys and unpredictable shops. Poultry hung upside-down on rails; fish lay on slabs, glassy-eyed; racks of flattened denims gave way to shelves of soiled paperbacks. Even the fresh vegetables were going limp in the humid atmosphere. The sequence of shops in each row was so arbitrary that it was hard to remember where you were, and yet the whole place felt unified and enclosed. The heavily filtered light made it seem like the floor of a murky tank.

I rounded a corner for what may have been the third or fourth time, and stopped in front of a café. Inside three isolated customers were fixed in a state of arrest over their cups of tea. I looked through the glass-panelled door, past its once-white net curtains, to the mirror behind the counter. The man had his back to me. He appeared to be engrossed in choosing something from a plastic showcase – a bun or a sandwich perhaps – but because of the mirror I could see his face clearly. We were much the same type, and I should find it hard to describe him. He raised his eyes to my reflection with no flicker of acknowledgement before taking his tea into the most recessed part of the room. I passed on, anxious now to get back outside.

*

Although I'd recently got to the stage when I had to give lectures myself rather than listen to other people's, I made an effort not to miss a particular seminar which was relevant to the research I was supposed to be doing. It was held in another college, not my own. As soon as I sat down I realized that she was already there, in the front row. It was the last of the series. Had she been in previous weeks? I don't think so – I would have noticed. A blackboard covered with indecipherable signs was propped against the wall nearest her, left over from a previous class.

He came in hurriedly at the last moment and sat in the seat next to her – one of the few remaining empty. As he did so, she turned her head a little to his side and shifted her position. Perhaps they knew each other already, slightly at least, or perhaps not. She ran her hand through her hair now and then while taking notes. They both seemed attentive to what the speaker was saying, though I was less so than usual.

Neither contributed to the formal discussion but they began to talk to each other quietly at the end, presumably about some point raised in it, and stayed, sitting together, until I was the only other person still there. The lecturer had picked up his notes and gone. I couldn't think of an excuse to linger, but I loitered on the grass outside, studying the label under an old climbing rose which was just beginning to flower. In a few minutes they passed me, murmuring in their earnest but subdued way, before passing through the gate into the sunlit street.

*

I sometimes worked in the college library because I needed to refer to some old books confined to it. In the bay where I sat I was faced by shelves of leather-bound folios whose gold titles on the worn spines gleamed dimly in certain lights. The building was deserted – the students were either taking examinations or out enjoying themselves because they were over – and I found the quiet slightly unnerving. The traffic noise outside seemed unusually distant. I looked out of the window often. The texts on which I was trying to concentrate hadn't survived the centuries through any compelling interest of their own, and their inertia seemed contagious.

The quadrangle outside was paved with stone except for some formal beds with herbs and a few straggling roses in them, which already had black spot. Each bed had a low hedge of clipped box round its perimeter; the hot sun brought out its smell so that it just reached me through the open window. On the far side there was a seventeenth-century arcade, a sort of baroque cloister. From where I sat, one floor up, most of it was in deep shadow; I could only have seen people walking along it if they did so at the outer edge.

It isn't difficult to fall asleep in libraries, especially in the afternoon. I heard the sound of footsteps before I woke fully to them, and was just in time to glimpse a figure moving away from me at the farther end of the arcade. All I could see was the lower half of a long light-coloured skirt which trailed slightly. I couldn't tell if it was really her, nor whether she had a companion on the far invisible side, on silent soles. But the tempo of her walk, the metronomic clack-clack of her heels on the stone slabs, seemed familiar. It was too late to follow, to find out where she was going or whether she was alone: by the time I'd have got downstairs and across to the other side she would have vanished, the space empty as before.

*

Two or three days later I was sitting with my colleagues in the room in which we usually had official meetings. It was always sombre, even sepulchral, an effect emphasized by the three tall

8

windows slit into the dark interior walls. It was often hard to attend to what was going on because of the inherent tedium of the business, especially when it was bright outside. I had latterly felt increasingly detached from the proceedings anyway, and tried to sit where I could see out on to the green expanse of grass, and the trees beyond.

We were half-way through the agenda when she crossed my field of vision, limited as it was by the narrowness of the window, and then recrossed it a few minutes later. She sat on the grass at intervals, remaining within the frame or partly so, the sunlight catching the white braid on her dress and on the broad-brimmed straw hat which kept her face in shadow. She seemed to be waiting for somebody. Each time she moved out of view I waited for her uncertain return. Finally she settled further off, took a book out of her bag, and began to read.

I became aware of an awkward silence in the room and felt the gaze of others. The chairman had asked me a question which I hadn't heard, and which embarrassingly had to be repeated. When I was free to look out again, she'd gone.

*

When it was as hot as it had now become I liked to go to the botanical gardens because of the water-lilied pool at the centre. The low stone rim was broad enough to sit on. The still water both reflected the heat and refreshed it. The sense of the south was intensified by the aromatic rock plants near by, and by the pines at a further distance; there was a strong smell of box. This privileged and unreal micro-climate was presumably due to the old brick walls of unusual height which protected it. In the brown water of the pool the carp gleamed enigmatically as they slowly emerged from and then returned to the obscurity beneath the floating leaves that roofed their world.

After basking in the sun for a while I felt I'd like yet more warmth, and I made for the hothouses in whose close humidity luxuriated species otherwise too exotic to survive this far north.

I opened the glass-panelled door, the hot air on my face, and immediately saw the two of them behind the first bay of staging. She was looking down at some strangely formed plants standing in pots at waist-height. He looked searchingly at her face, trying to read it. I got the impression that he had just said something that was sufficiently intense or serious enough in its implications for her to need time to adjust to it. She put one hand under some green fronds to support them, and brushed them lightly with the fingers of the other hand. They didn't look up as I closed the door quietly and retreated.

*

— I really need to see you, soon. Can I come round tonight? Would you mind if I came round?
— No, but I've got a lot to do. Can't we leave it?
— I could give you a ring. Shall I ring tomorrow, in the morning?
— I may not be in.
— I could ring early, if that's all right.
— I can't stop you ringing.

*

A week later I had my first opportunity. It was at a recital given by a celebrated pianist whose programme, despite his age, was long and taxing. The years seemed to have taught him a touching economy of effort. He sat at the keyboard in apparent repose, the authority of his performance unaccompanied by mannerism or grimace, playing some passages with his eyes shut, as if he had suddenly lost his sight. Such impassivity helped one's own concentration, so that I wasn't distracted by the features of the hall — its heavily framed portraits and its carved wood-panelling — nor made restive by the pressure of too many people on too warm an evening. It wasn't only the notes that spoke, but the silences between them.

I was near enough to her to see how absolutely still she remained, her hands lying inertly in her lap, the palms turned upwards, as if their power to move or even to feel had been withdrawn so that she might receive the music without reserve or defence. Only the slightest rise and fall of her breast showed that she breathed. This combination of suspense and extreme attention continued during the great set of variations that ended the programme. She held her head at exactly the same angle throughout, slightly to one side – perhaps one ear was more acute than the other. Neither of us clapped at the work's close as everyone else did. When she looked up at the elaborate ceiling I saw that her eyes brimmed.

She only began to leave her seat when the rest of the audience had gone. I watched her walk slowly out of the hall door and start to descend the stairs to the ground below. As I got up to go myself I realized she'd left her bag behind. I caught up with her as she was about to disappear through the gate into the street. 'I think this must be yours – it was under your chair,' I explained lamely. I wanted to talk about the concert, hoping this would lead to other things, so that I might find out something real about her. She smiled, and her eyes, still bright, rested on me briefly, but she said nothing. She took the bag and, with the same air of abstraction, walked away, leaving me standing in the close evening air.

*

I began to spend more and more time wandering about the streets. My days felt longer than ever, and in a sense they were so since it was midsummer; they always had gaps in them which I didn't know what to do with. I developed different circuits and varied them ingeniously from day to day, but there were limits to the city's variety, and I often got back weary at having seen nothing new.

I couldn't make any progress with the book I was trying to write; the whole project had become superfluous and futile. I tried to justify my increased daily mileage by telling myself that it gave me more thinking time, but it didn't work out like that. What I really hoped for was that my activity would in some way make

11

something happen, or that one day I'd see something which would clarify the situation, but my patrols went on being in every sense pedestrian.

I paid particular attention to the alleys of the market, paused often in front of shop windows whose contents I knew by heart, and began to recognize one or two other equally driven walkers whose beats intersected mine. In bookshops (which I thought of as likely places) the assistants kept an eye on me since I came in almost every day without even buying a paperback. The length of my excursions meant that by the home stretch I was usually exhausted, my shoes catching on the uneven paving-stones, sometimes making me stumble.

Once, when this happened, and when in consequence my eyes were fixed on the unreliable ground, I brushed against a woman walking in the opposite direction. Muttering an instinctive apology, I turned round as I straightened up and saw from her receding back who it was. The hem of her long skirt still dragged, and in her left hand she carried a shopping basket with a French loaf sticking out of it. The sound of her footsteps was suddenly drowned by a car accelerating. I could hardly have run back and overtaken her: what could I have said? Did she realize it was me?

*

I picked up the phone to ring a colleague about an academic matter I should have dealt with weeks ago, and heard voices — a crossed line, presumably. It sounded like them but I couldn't be sure, nor could I make out what they were talking about. Of course I hadn't heard her voice clearly yet, but I knew exactly what it would be like. As I listened, the accent and intonation already seemed familiar; I recognized the timbre, despite the phone's restricted frequencies. His voice, on the other hand, was disconcerting and hard to place. It reminded me a bit of the first time I heard my own voice played back on tape.

*

12

– I got so worried when you were late.

– You shouldn't have worried.

– I thought you might have had an accident. People do have accidents – I knew someone who fell under a bus. It could have been you.

– Well, I arrived in the end.

– I know it's stupid to worry, but I can't seem to stop it.

– There's no need to worry, not about me.

– I do worry, all the same. Please take care, promise me you'll take care.

*

I was having so little luck that I began to include other places not yet on my itineraries which might possibly yield results. One afternoon I suddenly thought of the supermarket. Everyone has to shop sometimes, even those who are catered for institutionally, as I – and perhaps she – was. It was in a part of the city where I didn't often go, and I hadn't chosen a good time. It was crowded with people who knew what they wanted and where to find it. I had to fall back as they pounced on the exact flavour of yoghurt preferred or unerringly singled out the favoured brand of biscuit. As I went up and down between the stacked shelves the congregated mass of foodstuff began to oppress me. The fresh vegetables were at least green and unprocessed, but I looked away from all the cuts of prepared meat, sealed in their transparent packs like specimen organs, nor did I relish the walls of butter and other fats. Suppose the refrigeration failed, so that the bricks began to lose their shape and slid to the floor? The juxtaposition of incompatible goods – dogfoods and household bleach, for instance – made me queasy, as I imagined one being poured over the other. But everybody else seemed at ease and at home.

At the checkout I saw a young woman waiting behind a loaded trolley on which a grubby and fractious boy was sitting. She looked tired and bedraggled, but her slack body breathed content. When her chap came up to join her, brandishing a packet of the kind

13

of detergent she wanted, she looked up at him with placid love. 'Found it in the end then?' she said.

I realized that I was empty-handed and had nothing to declare to the cashier. I went back and collected a bottle of wine at random – it turned out to be a type that I didn't like and never drank – and got out as soon as I could. Of her – or of him – there was of course no sign. It was obviously a stupid idea in the first place.

*

I began to fear that I was losing my touch. Towards the end of another expedition I approached a parked car with a woman sitting in it, her bowed head resting on the steering-wheel. From behind I could only see the hair but I felt it might be her – for a moment I was really sure it was her. The car windows were closed and the passing traffic was noisy, but as I got nearer I could see from the tremor of her shoulders that she was sobbing. When I drew level on the pavement she looked up abruptly and stared at me through the glass, but I don't think she actually saw me. Then she turned away, found some tissues in the pocket of the car, dabbed her eyes, switched on the radio, and drove off sharply without checking her rear mirror. There was no resemblance whatever.

*

I've been to so many open-air performances of Shakespeare in college gardens that I only went to this particular production of *The Tempest* out of a vague sense of loyalty to the director whom I knew. But the evening was warm and still, and as the daylight faded the clear young voices, amateurish as they were, spoke the verse well enough to convey its extraordinary suggestiveness afresh. I was specially astonished by Ariel's warning to the conspirators that they might as well 'wound the loud winds, or with bemocked-at stabs /Kill the still-closing waters' as try to diminish his power. The words stayed with me for days; I felt I'd never heard them before.

As the costumed figures of the student actors moved with

touching artlessness under the artificial light – softer and less flat than the dusk it gradually superseded – they became more defined, more beautiful. The Prospero was scarcely older than his daughter, but since he often appeared on part of the old city wall above the main acting area, the height gave him an authority he was otherwise bound to lack. When he began to show Ferdinand and Miranda what his spirits could do in the masque, I suddenly realized who was playing Ceres. Her hair was appropriately corn-coloured. She stood on a small rostrum, the weathered stone behind her; a lamp hung in a nearby tree shone through the branches and lent her face a pale radiance. Her expression had its usual grave impassivity. When the masque abruptly dispersed one of the spirits threw a black cloth over her head to make her invisible, and led her away. I looked in the programme and at last read her name. She didn't appear with the others in the curtain call. Perhaps her part was so small that she didn't feel it worth her while to wait, or perhaps she had something else arranged. I scanned the audience carefully, but he didn't seem to be there.

I went again to the next, and final, performance. A light breeze stirred the leaves during her speeches so that – although they kept their soft-voiced clarity – they sounded more remote than before. Although you weren't supposed to take photographs during the play itself, I did get a shot of the assembled cast (which this time included her) at the end. I know nothing about cameras; mine was supposed to be automatic, but for some reason the picture didn't come out.

I spoke to the director afterwards and, with elaborate casualness, asked him about her. She'd come in at the last minute because someone else had dropped out; he couldn't tell me much about her except what college she was at. His impression was that she was doing research of some kind. It was something to go on.

*

I rang her college and explained that I wanted to get in touch with one of their postgraduates, adding defensively that it was an academic matter. They weren't interested in the elaborate justification for my enquiry, and gave me her address without even asking my name. Encouraged, I phoned the university offices to find out which faculty she belonged to and what degree she was working for. Again, there was no difficulty. Oddly enough, her topic was not too distant from my own interests, neglected as these had recently become.

But even with this information I still held back. I knew the street she lived in, just as I knew all the other streets within walking distance, but I didn't immediately include it in my daily excursions. I didn't want to risk another chance encounter, unprepared. And anyway I needed to know more about him, and what was between them. If I didn't observe them, how could I find anything out?

*

I looked into the mirror to try to see what he looked like when he looked at her. I gazed at my own face as if it was hers that I saw, wanting to make her image swim into focus and superimpose itself on mine. But as soon as I took my eyes off myself I could no longer see myself looking at myself, and therefore couldn't see how he or I might look to her. The stupidity of the exercise didn't make it any the less frustrating. What would it be like to be looked at by eyes as full of longing as I tried to make mine show? I realized that I should only see that if she were really there and not the mirror, or if she and he were really there and I could see them, myself unseen.

*

– I do love you. I love you so much.
– So you keep saying.
– Do you mind my saying it?
– You needn't say it so often.
– But I feel it all the time.
– I know that.
– Well then.
– I feel you say it to make me say I love you.

16

– Don't you want to say you love me?

– Sometimes.

*

I had some difficulty in persuading the porter that I could be trusted
with the key of the college tower, but he gave way eventually. At
ground-level the inside was simply a square space with scattered
odds and ends on the stone-flagged floor – lawn-mowing equipment,
apparently abandoned, a garden-seat needing repair, even a pile of
discarded hymnbooks. On the second storey a single wooden chair
with a broken cane seat had been placed near a slit in the wall
through which the garden could be observed. Perhaps someone
had come up here regularly, to keep watch.

The stone staircase got steeper with each flight. It was hard to
pull back the bolt on the underside of the trap-door to the roof,
and the trap itself was so heavy that I had to heave it up by putting
my back under it. As I did so the sudden burst of heat and light
made me dizzy for a few seconds.

I moved forward gingerly across the roof to its edge, holding on
to the waist-high battlements tightly as I surveyed the city. The grey
stone was warm but roughened by weather so that its surface was
pitted and uneven. One or two nearby spires made me look up, but
most of the roofs round me were lower than I was. As I blinked in the
glare their varied geometrical shapes seemed first to blur and then
flatten into one plane without depth of field, like a cubist picture
of the most doctrinaire kind. This upper world seemed too arid to
support any life except that of birds, such as the two pigeons who
looked at me sidelong from the opposite side of the tower. When
I moved towards them they took off, but heavily, as if it was an
effort to become airborne. The flap of their wings was unexpectedly
loud, perhaps because most other noises were attenuated by the
height, although some sounds detached themselves from the general
hum with unmuffled clarity: an ambulance siren, a stray shout,
unexplained bangs (as if a metal door had fallen flat), a sharp report
(a shot perhaps, or a burst tyre).

17

This side of the tower faced another college whose flag was flying at half-mast. I wondered who had died – whether some kindly scholar had passed peacefully away among his books, or whether one of the students, in debt, on drugs, or just rejected, had ended it all. I made myself look straight down to the narrow lane which ran between the two buildings. The faces of the people walking along it were hard to make out because the angle of vision was not flat enough. The lane was barred to traffic, but bicycles were allowed. I'd almost given up when a couple appeared pedalling alongside, each with one hand on the handlebar and one on the other's shoulder. I gripped the stone hard as I bent over it, hoping it wouldn't suddenly crumble, trying to see if it was them, but I was too high up to be sure.

I began to feel the sun on top of my head. Going down, there was no hand-rail on the outside of the spiral to help you keep your balance. I let down the trap on my back, and sat on the stair as I again struggled with the bolt. It was dark after the brightness outside, and for a moment I thought I was going to pitch forward. I didn't want to risk standing up, so I negotiated the first flight by sitting on each step in turn, lowering myself from one to the next; then I turned round and descended on all fours until I reached the ground. I stood up, and leant against the wall, with my forehead touching the stone, still cool at this level.

When I took the key back to the lodge, I saw that my hands were covered in dust.

*

Some days later, on my rounds, I was about to pass a cinema when, on impulse, I decided to go in. The heat had now become so settled that the idea of escaping from it into the cool dark seemed attractive, whatever the film. I like early evening performances anyway, when the house is still thin and the seats on either side of you empty. And then, when you come out, the street-lamps are on, and you can feel that another day is almost done with.

I only realized they were there during the interval, when the lights undimmed. They were sitting a few rows in front of me but at a diagonal, so that I could see them in profile as they watched the screen and I watched them. The film had been made in the Fifties, a relatively commercial work by a continental director later famous for his austerity. It was about an enigmatic girl leading a double life, and included a bedroom scene that had caused some scandal in its day although it now seemed almost decorous. I looked at them with particular concentration as one of the heroes began to undress the heroine; the actress panted delicately as her breasts were discovered by her lover, and by us. The subtitler tactfully gave up trying to render the accompanying murmurs.

They seemed neither embarrassed nor excited by what they saw. Their heads didn't incline or turn towards each other as far as I could make out, in the screen's reflected twilight. Admittedly they could have been holding hands, or his palm could have lain lightly on her thigh, so that by slight pressures they might anticipate or remind each other of analogous moments, but from where I was I couldn't check. On the other hand there was a stiffness in the way they sat which could have indicated some tension or reserve between them. I thought about going to the cloakroom through the door at the front of the stalls so as to be able to glance at them along the row as I returned, but in the event I left the cinema altogether.

Because I'd abandoned the programme half-way through it was still bright outside, but the streets smelt fresher. I walked back slowly, wishing for the first time since the heat-wave began that the weather would break.

*

By now every street I dragged myself along had become the site of some encounter so longed for that it seemed like a memory. There was no venue in the city centre where they might have met that I didn't keep my eye on, from time to time, knowing that I should catch up with them, sooner or later.

One lunchtime I looked through the window of a newly opened wine bar. He was threading his way between the tables until he came up to the one she was sitting at. He put the drinks down, and stood in

19

front of her. It was difficult to catch her expression because she had turned away from the light, but on his side there was a look of what might have been resentment. At any rate, when he raised his eyes to stare out of the window, straight at me, his face was set.

Perhaps my hunch in the cinema was right, perhaps not. I wished I knew how things stood.

*

— You hurt me so much when you say that.
— I have to say what I feel. You shouldn't ask me what I feel, if it upsets you.
— But how can you feel like that, after what's happened?
— I expect I feel like that because of what's happened. You shouldn't mind so much.
— How can I help minding?
— I can't help your minding.

*

I hadn't opened my diary for a long time; one day had become so like another that I was unsure of the date. I checked to see whether I'd forgotten some appointment, but the pages were blank for weeks ahead. Evidently I was not in demand, but then no one was at this time of year. Exams were over, schools on holiday, and most of my colleagues were away, leaving their colleges to the listless gaze of tourists.

I'd been at my desk so little that its chronic disorder was even greater than usual. I found several unopened envelopes; one of them contained an invitation for an evening already past, so I wasn't entirely forgotten. I shouldn't have felt like it anyway, not in my present state, but I ought to have replied. I might as well go round and apologize.

The house was in the one road I'd still been avoiding, opposite the address I'd been given by her college. I was let in by my friend's flat-mate, who was on the point of going out. I could wait if I liked. I wandered about the room, browsed through the bookshelves, and came to rest behind the desk which faced the window. It was covered with confused papers, much as mine was. Something stuck in the typewriter had been left in mid-paragraph, or rather – now that I looked at it more closely – in mid-sentence, as if the author had found himself imprisoned in his own syntax, and couldn't see how to get out.

I became aware of a flicker of movement in the blurred distance beyond the page. I looked up and out, and saw that the curtains of the wide first-floor window across the street had been partly closed against the afternoon sun. As I watched, a pale shape swam in the far recesses of the room. Then, after a pause, her white back came suddenly into focus as she moved into the space just behind the still-uncovered pane. There was a thin line across it below the shoulder blades. Standing for a moment within the frame, she put both hands behind her to undo the strap, before retreating once more.

As he sat on the side of the bed, she had the light behind her, coming towards him. He stretched out his hand to touch her breast; she kneeled; he brushed the nipple with his lips; she put her hand on his hair.

*

– Do you mind if I touch you?
– No, I don't mind.
– Do you like it when I touch you?
– I'm not sure. I'm not used to it.
– I touch you because I love you.
– I know you do.
– Do you mind my loving you?
– I don't think so.

*

Like other houses in the area – originally built for large Victorian families and their many servants – it was now divided up, and without what I had learned from my vigil on the other side it would have been difficult to know which room was hers. The front door yielded easily, and I made for the staircase. It was wide enough to make the ribbon of worn carpet in the middle look almost as thin as a tightrope; it rose steeply to a banistered landing like a balcony.

I worked out which of the three doors facing me to try, but I had no idea what to say when, and if, she opened it. My first knock was too diffident and, worrying that it might not have been heard, I repeated it more firmly. I listened for signs of life; perhaps she was out. At last I heard the sound of someone moving, but I couldn't tell which room it came from. I was about to knock for the third time, my fist raised to shoulder-height, when the door abruptly opened.

She was in a dressing-gown, just pulled on. Her feet on the boarded floor of the threshold were bare. She blinked at me, her eyes a little swollen with sleep, but said nothing. It wasn't her, but something about her face, the way she stood, reminded me of her. I explained who I'd come to see. She opened the door wider to let me in, and then disappeared. I heard a tap turned on, and then off. I went across to the window, and looked out from the space I had looked into. Nothing was happening in the room opposite: I was here and not there. The door behind me reopened.

'Sorry about that,' she said, with mock ruefulness, 'but I like to rest in the afternoon when it's as hot as this, don't you? That's what they do in the south. Would you like some tea, or coffee?'

She had put on the nearest clothes to hand – jeans, T-shirt, no bra. Her bright hair was still uncombed, and she kept pushing it back as she bent down to the kettle on the hearth by the gas fire, dusty and long unlit. We said nothing until she passed me my cup.

'You do look puzzled. It's quite simple really. The person you want is my sister. We're supposed to be rather alike, though I don't see it myself. She went off to France yesterday and I'm moving in while she's away. I'll give you her address if it's any help. She gets fed up with this place in the summer, but I like it. What about you – are you going or staying?'

I said I'd stay for a second cup at least. She talked easily, and was easy to talk to. I had hardly spoken to anyone properly for so long that I began to feel almost light-headed. There was something about her which excited me. It was partly the resemblance of course, even though it was frustratingly intermittent. A turn of the head, the play of the light on her forehead or cheek made me think, for an amazed moment, that it really was her at last; a second later, it obviously wasn't. But it was also the way she sat, or rather slumped, in her low chair, her hands at rest with the palms turned half-upwards, except when she pushed back her hair. When she raised an arm to do this I was conscious of the way it lifted her breast on that side.

After another half-hour I made myself stand up to go. She reached for a book lying near by on the faded carpet. I turned back at the door.

'See you,' I said.

After looking at me with her half-smile for longer than I expected, she found her page and began to read.

*

I gave up my walks. What was the point? There was no chance of my coming across her now. If I were to spot him it would reassure me that they hadn't gone off together, but that was hardly motive enough.

I spent more and more time in my room, trying to work but mostly drinking, not copiously but steadily, sip by sip. As I read I kept getting to the bottom of the page without having taken anything in. It's not easy for someone like me to lose all interest in the printed word, but I managed it. When it began to get dark outside, in the late summer evening, I didn't draw the curtains; my room was high up and not overlooked. The clouds seemed on the increase but the rain they promised still failed to arrive, the next day turning out as warm as before, although hazy first thing.

I felt increasingly cut off, up there. It seemed as if I hardly knew anyone any more. This could hardly be the case. I moved the bottle aside, took some file-paper out of the drawer, and started writing down names. I kept a separate sheet for each category: personal friends, professional colleagues, students I'd taught, my immediate family, my remoter relations, and so on. I put down some of the already dead, although strictly speaking they were out of it. I also included the two women I'd been seriously in love with (or so it had seemed), as well as a few more that I'd been close to. None of them cared about me now, as far as I knew, nor did I still miss them.

After an hour or so the register had become quite extensive, but the longer it grew the less consoling it became. I realized that I didn't want, at that moment, to see a single one of them. I would have crossed the street to avoid them, but they had already begun to anticipate me, moving off, taking bits of my life with them.

*

I didn't feel too good the next day. I half-drew the curtains because the light outside seemed brighter than ever, and after lunch lay on my sofa. I wasn't sure that I'd really heard the knock, and waited until it was repeated. I couldn't pretend I wasn't there so I raised my voice to answer, but didn't get up.

As she stood framed by the doorway in the dimmest part of the room, I thought for a moment that she really was the other, but as she came forward the image stabilized. She looked down at me with her usual wry expression.

'I'm going for a drive in the country. I thought you might like to come. You look as if some fresh air might do you good.'

It was true that I hadn't been out of the city for weeks. When I had a car I often used it to get away, but it had begun to need expensive repairs and I had given it up.

We left the main road for a deeper country of narrowing lanes, the verges high with grass and cow parsley not yet mown.

'Where are we going?'

'To the downs. I've discovered a spot where no one ever goes. I like empty places, don't you?'

24

We didn't pause on the crest of the upland to look back over the plain, but drove on until we reached the bottom of a wide green bowl, the land rising to its rim all round us, open to the cloudless sky but cutting off further view. There were no farmhouses that I could see, and only one barn.

We crossed three fields towards the edge of a copse, carrying our picnic and a rug; I spread it where the grass was thickest. We faced the sun, still high, with the trees behind us, their leaves hardly moving in the heat. I walked on up a chalky track, but it soon petered out. When I returned she was sunbathing, her T-shirt off and her skirt pulled up to her thighs, her eyes closed.

I lay down next to her and shut mine too. It was peaceful but not silent. The noise of a tractor, increasing or lessening as it went up and down a distant field, merged with the indefinable general hum of summer. A light aircraft buzzed slowly across the sky as it used to when I was a boy. The sounds were beginning to drift away from me when it grew darker behind my eyelids; she was kneeling beside me, so that I was in her shade. She leant over and began to undo my shirt, her breasts close to my face.

'Are you sure this is a good idea?'

'Why not? Do you mind?'

Later she said, 'I love days like this.'

We slept, I on my back, she on her side, her bare arm across me, heavy on my skin. When I woke I tried to pick out the lark tirelessly singing somewhere above, but it was too high to see. I wondered again whether I ought to have my eyes tested. I've always hated the idea of glasses.

'Don't frown,' she said, smoothing my forehead with her fingers.

When we parted, back in the city, she put her hands on my shoulders and said, in a tone that seemed partly ironic and partly not, 'Well, did you enjoy your drive in the country?'

I kissed her as gently as I could, not knowing what to say, or where I was, now.

*

25

The noise became more distinct as the competing sound of the rush-hour traffic began to die down. I couldn't think what it was until I realized it must be the city's famous fair, held every year at this time in its wide central street. But once I was in the middle of it I wasn't as deafened as I'd expected because the loudspeaker nearest to me drowned out the others. In any case it was mainly the beat that came through; you couldn't hear any words amongst the laughs and shouts of the fairgoers, the clatter of the roundabouts, and the throb of their generators.

I didn't try any of the rides myself, not wanting to have to hold on, but I stood and watched. The gravity of the little children circling sedately on the nursery roundabout showed they knew they had to take their treat seriously; it was past their bedtime. The boys tumbling on to the mat at the bottom of the helter-skelter chute were more nonchalant: there was nothing to it. I should have liked to follow them as they went up inside the tower for another go, but thought better of it. The galloping horses were the same as I remembered them. It made no difference who their riders were; their mouths remained open in unchanging rictus, sharply reined back, teeth bared. Their eyes flickered under the revolving lights, as if panic would set in once they broke free from the rise and fall which kept them endlessly reinforcing themselves as they came round again and again.

Even so, I preferred their regularity to the random collisions of the dodgems. How you steered the cars seemed to make little difference to where they went. Now and then they swarmed together and had to be broken up by the men who collected the money, standing on the rubber bumpers and then leaping from one vehicle to another, never missing their footing, equal to any contingency.

As one of these liberators spun a car round and set it free, I glimpsed the faces of its driver and the girl with him, on the far side of the floor. It was difficult to be sure because of the flashing lights that were taking over from the fading day, but it looked like them all right. He was impassive as usual, but she was excited — a different person, almost, from the one I'd been with myself in another car, so recently. As she laughed and touched his arm my view was blacked out by some heavies in motor-cycle gear who pushed in front of me.

Should I keep an eye on them, or make off quickly lest they should see me? That might be awkward for her, and I certainly didn't want to face him. Going home, it occurred to me that at least he couldn't be with both of them at once.

My room was cool and quiet. I drank some water, polishing the glass first, so that both container and contained were equally transparent. I realized with relief that the logic of the situation could not be more simple. If he was still here, then the obvious thing for me to do was to go there. After all, she'd given me the address. She shouldn't be too hard to find, even in another country.

*

On the other side of the ferry's plate-glass window the green sea creamed into foam here and there, but it was calm. In the cafeteria two boys sitting at the next table lashed into their sausages and chips while their mother looked on with pride. I nibbled at a roll and salad, and sipped some wine. I was all right, for the moment, but I felt worried about being queasy later; I'm not what is called a good sailor. I screened myself behind a newspaper lest I should be spotted by someone I knew and have to explain myself, although it was hardly likely.

As I sat over my coffee, trying to kill time, I began to feel a little light in the head. It wasn't so much the sight or sensation of the swell as the increasing noise all round me – the chatter of voices, the public announcements in badly accented French, the clash of cutlery and banging of trays. When I stood up I was distinctly dizzy. I steadied myself on the way out by holding on to the rail, as if the boat really was pitching enough to put one off balance.

It was a relief to surface into the air, but I'd forgotten how breezy it is in mid-channel, even on fine days. I did an almost complete circuit before finding a sheltered corner, at the stern. The seagulls hung above the ship's receding wake. After a while the unceasing play of their grey and white against the green made me blink; I had to look away, and refocus.

I had to find somewhere to lie down. The narrow passages of the cabin deck were deserted. I pushed tentatively at several doors; one of them yielded. No one inside, no belongings lying about, no polythene bags of duty-free booze. I rested on the bunk, flat on my back; my breathing became steadier. There were no voices down here, inside or out. The pulse of the ship's engines was reassuring, despite the occasional shudder in its rhythm, and the creaks and vibrations of the cabin itself were like the faint sounds one hears in the house when alone, at night. I began to feel safe, in my little cell. Below me the battered French car I'd bought was waiting, looking even smaller than it was because of the juggernaut behind. I would have to get to it in good time to rescue it, when we landed, but that wouldn't be for quite a while yet.

As I closed my eyes, I seemed myself to be floating within the vessel that was itself afloat.

*

The hotel must have been built not long after the war. The room at the back would always have been dingy, and had got dingier. The wardrobe and bedside tables were flimsy reproductions of period pieces. Over the bed hung a banal picture of a girl in a spring orchard. As the shutters opened on to three similar walls there was no outlook. At the bottom of the well there was a pile of crates full of empty bottles.

The meal was a serious affair, designed for local tastes, not tourists. The diners ignored each other and followed the slow evolution of the exacting menu with respect, contemplating each course with a sigh when it arrived, and then working methodically through it. They drank their wine and mineral water with an air of abstraction, in no hurry to break the collective calm by getting up from the table. I was the first to go.

28

I thought about walking round the town, but I hadn't got far before I gave it up. These streets could hold nothing for me.

*

The large bed was unexpectedly comfortable. I sat up against the headboard and began to watch television. I couldn't tell what stage the film had got to, but as I joined it a young woman, seen from above, was crossing the square of some *bastide* in the south, threading her way through the parked cars. The camera then tracked her at ground-level, though still from a distance, as she walked along under the stone arcade. She turned into a side street and went into a *boulangerie*. When she emerged, putting a loaf into her bag and looking uncertainly from left to right, I wished I could have frozen the frame so as to study what it was about her that had changed. It wasn't just that her hair was cut differently and that her face was tauter and more tanned. It was rather that the eyes now seemed both to take in what was outside her and to reflect what was within. On her way back to the square she met another woman, and at first I couldn't understand why her voice had altered too; it had been dubbed, of course. Presumably her French wasn't good enough.

I hadn't thought of her for some time, although I knew she'd had some early professional success. I'd had to teach her the Shakespeare paper and it hadn't worked out too well: her essays were usually perfunctory because she'd been busy rehearsing. After reading them out she didn't have much to say, and nor did I. She attracted me, but I don't think I interested her; at any rate, I couldn't make her out. I never knew where role ended and reality began. Perhaps she didn't either.

After some scenes with other characters which meant little to me because I hadn't grasped the plot, she reappeared in the last sequence. She was looking out of the upstairs window of an isolated house in the local style. It was late so that, with the light in the room behind her, she was almost in silhouette. She pulled in the shutters and, turning back into the interior where the camera was now waiting for her, walked past it, shedding clothes as she went. She came out of the bathroom with a towel round her which she discarded as she got into bed, leaving it to lie on the boarded floor.

She put out the light and lay on her back in the gloom, listening. The camera came to rest on her still face; her eyes were closed. Despite the sound of the car's approach and the slam of its doors, the camera kept its gaze on the bed. After a pause he lifted the cover and stealthily lay down beside her. She turned towards him, half asleep, not opening her eyes.

'C'est vraiment toi?' she murmured, in the voice that was not her voice.

'Bien sûr, c'est moi. Je te dérange, peut-être?' he replied, with tender irony.

'Mais non, pas du tout.'

She explored his face with the tips of her fingers, as if she were blind, before allowing herself to be enfolded, beginning to yield, before the fade.

*

The south was certainly getting nearer. The land was drier and stonier, hedges less common. Now and then I passed straggling vines and blocks of maize; more and more sunflowers turned their blackening dials the way I was going. The road led straight to the horizon where another village had sited its church so that it stayed in your view for a long time before you reached it. Regularly spaced trees along the roadside laid down bars of shade; I drove through a grid of light and dark. The warning splashes of white paint on their trunks made me blink, and as the car went by it sounded like successive waves foaming on shingle at short intervals. The road flowed underneath with extraordinary smoothness, as if it was moving rather than the vehicle. Owing to some trick of the light the leaves reflected in the sloping windscreen seemed to pass over and behind me in a kind of slipstream. I tried to concentrate on what was ahead, but the absence of traffic in the hot and sleepy hour after lunch provided nothing to alert me.

The engine must have stalled on impact, but the damage wasn't serious – not even a puncture. Fortunately the ditch where the highway had unexpectedly swerved was wide and shallow, and had long since dried out. I wasn't worried about a dent or two, as long as the car was in good enough shape to continue.

I lay on the ground until I'd got my breath back, and the day had cooled a little. When I got going again I was on my guard against any more lapses.

*

I'd been more shaken up than I realized at the time and, as I got nearer, I took it more easily. I was increasingly uncertain about what to do, exactly, when I did arrive. I avoided the main routes, made detours, and wandered off down side roads. Late in the afternoon I followed a sign pointing to the river. A long strip of rough grass on the bank was backed by a double line of poplars. I left the car in their shade, with the others already parked there. The land on this side was flat, but opposite the rock reared straight up from the water's edge, furrowed horizontally by the torrents of some distant age, its grey-white surface made the more staring by the dark green of the water sliding beneath it. Some anglers at the cliff's foot looked oddly diminished: the river must be wider than it seemed. I wondered how deep it was in the middle. The few swimmers had already come in, drying themselves in the still warm sun.

I wandered along the shore where the water was shallow and clear. Shoals of tiny and translucent fish, like splinters of glass, darted impetuously among the stone and then suddenly froze, holding their little lengths against the current. They scattered at the approach of a large dog which splashed clumsily up to me. 'Viens ici, Axel!' shouted its owner, loudly enough to prompt an echo from the far side. 'Axel!' he called again, with resigned irritation. 'Axel,' replied the cliff, more obedient than the dog was.

At this late stage in the season there weren't enough people to make it crowded, and I stayed on. At first I felt awkward because I had nothing with me – no book to read, no food or drink –

but I sat it out, gazing round at discreet intervals to see what the others were doing, watching the shadows lengthen. Everyone took a long time to pack up. The children were no sooner out of their bathing things than they rushed off again in all directions, unpredictably, like butterflies, and had to be recaptured by their fathers, pretending to be monsters. The women smiled as they put the picnic things away. Did I ever have a day like that? I couldn't recall one. Fixing canoes to the cars' roof-racks was another ritual, each rope tested and re-knotted as if for a long journey, not just the short trip back to the campsite. The old man who'd been sitting in the shade refolded his newspaper for the last time; his wife put aside her knitting with regret. They went down to the water together and inspected it, exchanging glances of indecipherable meaning, before they too drove off.

Apart from an immobile fisherman on the other side I was the only person left. I could hear the papery rustle of the leaves in the trees now. I lay on my back and stared at the sky, its blue less brilliant than it was; I lay on my stomach and observed some ants. Then I went down to the shore again, and threw in some pebbles. It was hard to tell the difference between the little plop they made, as they fell into the water, and the sound of the fish jumping for flies, further out, breaking the surface from below. A pair of small birds skimmed the river from side to side at speed, and then disappeared.

When the sun was lost behind the rock the colour of the water changed, first to brown and then, in places, almost to black. I found a heavy stick, bleached by the weather, almost a metre long, and threw it into the middle. Its whiteness showed up well on the darkening stream before it was carried away, too far for me to see any more, in the failing light.

*

I sat in the chair by the open window in the room I'd taken above the café-bar. It was noisy because it overlooked the main street, but I didn't mind since it gave me a long view of the opposite pavement; I could keep an eye on the near-side too, if I leaned out. There was always a chance that she would pass by on her way to the shops or the bank or the post office – or to a restaurant, to meet someone.

I'd decided not to risk a direct approach at first: what if she just walked away, as before? And anyway I might not be calm enough – face to face, after so long – to know what to say. Best to do some research, and work something out accordingly.

The village she was staying in was further up the valley, ten minutes' drive away. She was bound to come to the little town where I was from time to time, and then our paths would cross once more as they used to do, in the city. The twice-weekly street market was an obvious possibility, and I'd spent most of the morning hovering round crowded stalls loaded with the vivid produce of the south. I had to buy some fruit for myself in the end. That evening's concert – the last of the summer's special events – would surely be another opportunity: with her love of music she would hardly neglect it.

The church was larger than I expected, given the size of the place. When I got there, a bit early, the audience was sparse, but people went on drifting in well after the programme's advertised start. There seemed little sense of urgency among the musicians either, when they finally appeared; they tuned up wearily, as if they'd already had a long day. I had plenty of time to keep watch on the desk, inside the wooden door, where tickets were sold. I found a good position next to a massive pillar behind which it was easy to retreat.

When the concert eventually got going she still hadn't arrived, but I felt sure the music must draw her in. I sat forward, covered my face with my hands, and willed it to reach her. The playing in the first movement was ragged, but in the Adagio the orchestra suddenly found its concentration, hearing and answering its own sound, as it hung in the great space above us. If only she could have heard it, it might have changed everything. I kept my eyes shut lest they should moisten, as hers had.

I was trying to pull myself together, braced by a now confident Scherzo, when the lights went out and the music fell apart. The

audience murmured, but not with alarm. They were used to
power-cuts at this time of year, when there was always a risk of
thunder, after the day's heat. Some illumination remained, from
the candles in front of a remote side-altar. Their faint gleam just
touched the gold of the harp and the silver of the soloist's flute. More
candles were being brought, and light would soon be restored.

I didn't wait for it, but went out into the refreshed air. The worn
steps down to the street were flecked with spots of rain. There were
a few more flashes and rumbles, before the storm retreated, and
the sky was dark again.

*

I couldn't wait for her any longer. I had to do something. I decided
to explore the valley where she was staying, and see the famous rock
which dominated it. Its grey face had cream-coloured patches where
flakes of stone had fallen off, at one time or another. The river had
worn away its base so much that, in theory, you could look over the
edge and see your reflection in the water beneath. I abandoned the
car, and as I climbed the smell of the box, growing in the crevices,
consoled me. The slopes were steep, but I breathed easily.

When I'd got to the top I moved carefully, step by step, towards
the unfenced edge until I could see the river, so far below. On the
opposite side was the usual grove of poplars, planted in straight
lines. Some of the leaves were beginning to turn; one or two of them
fluttered down. I shut my eyes because the sun was so bright, and
when I opened them again she was walking between the trees, near
the bank. The hat, the skirt, were the same. I called out to her,
to look up, but she couldn't have heard me.

*

After crying her name, he stepped forward into nothing. As he
fell from the cliff's height the air seemed to let him down gently
until the water closed over him, its glossy surface, a moment later,
showing no sign of agitation.

34

[2]

HONEYMOON

When he woke she was still asleep. He turned towards her stealthily, trying not to disturb the bedclothes, and began to look carefully at her head on the pillow. Although they had made love often enough before yesterday's marriage, they had never, for various reasons, been able to sleep together all night, so that this was the first time he'd been able to study her morning face. He thought of all the different dawns in which he'd now be able to see it in the endless future. In the hotel room the light was beginning to seep round the edges of the curtains, and the blank television screen was losing its earlier ashen pallor. Their clothes, which lay about on the carpet, were becoming more distinct.

As he looked again at her face he was dismayed to see the faintest of frown lines between her eyebrows. He'd always loved her open forehead and often smoothed her hair back from it, stroking her temples with his fingertips when she had a headache. It struck him that he couldn't have observed her closely enough if this detail had escaped him. Would the lines deepen with age? Yes, they were bound to, eventually, but probably not for a long time yet. At any rate this was the face he would see beside him every morning, and perhaps he would get so used to it that he wouldn't notice all the little changes – infinitesimal in themselves – that would make it, one day, almost unrecognizable. The same would be true of his own face of course, but that didn't matter so much because he wasn't beautiful to start with – not, at least, to himself. Perhaps she thought he was, but she had never said so.

He remembered the first time he'd ever seen her, at a concert. What had caught his attention, as he'd idly looked along the rows of his fellow-listeners as one does at concerts, was the rapt immobility of her expression. She hardly seemed to breathe. At the end of the performance everyone round her clapped enthusiastically, but she stayed still, although her eyes shone. She'd been so absorbed in what she'd just heard that on leaving she forgot her bag. Retrieving and restoring it, he'd been able to contrive their first meeting.

Her face had something of that stillness now, but because her eyes were covered by their still, slightly shadowed lids she seemed curiously, almost alarmingly, impassive. Her eyelashes were shorter than he had thought. When he had turned over in the night she'd been breathing heavily, but at the moment the movement of air was barely detectable. He gazed intently at her features as if he knew he would never see them again and wanted to memorize them. The chin had a slight scar on the left side, presumably more visible than usual because it was normally veiled by make-up. How had that happened? She had never told him; on the other hand, he had never asked. The upper lip showed a few fine hairs: would they become more conspicuous, in time, and would he mind? He wanted to kiss her but kept his mouth a few inches away, so that he could just feel her outgoing breath. It smelt of sleep and bed and staleness, and the intimate suggestiveness of it brought back the excitement of the night before. There had been a sense of release beyond his previous experience; marriage seemed to mean that you could let yourself go, at last. Would it always be as good – and had it been as good for her? She had opened herself to him so readily that he had been almost shocked, despite their former intimacies. She's mine now, he thought, with a sudden possessiveness, her body belongs to me.

He slowly pulled back the sheet to look at her more fully. She like him was naked because last night they had solemnly put on their nightclothes and then – standing on either side of the bed – had begun to laugh at the absurdity of it, and had taken them off again before plunging between the sheets. Her breasts were whiter than the rest of her skin: they'd been modestly covered up in the sun. On the shoulder too there was a thin pale line where the straps had been. He put his open mouth over her left nipple and touched it softly with the tip of his tongue.

She woke abruptly. For a brief moment which he was afterwards never able to forget she looked at him with the open eyes of complete surprise.

'Oh, it's you,' she said.

'Of course it's me,' he said. 'Who else would it be?'

'I'm glad it's you,' she said, as she pressed her body closer to his.

BEDROOM SCENE

They were reading in bed. It was already late because they had sat up to watch the play on television. She was half upright, her pillows between her back and the headboard, holding her script, trying to learn her lines in tomorrow's scene. He was lying down but with an extra pillow under his head, looking through a literary weekly. She knew he was irritable from the way he refolded it when he turned to another page.

'What's the matter?'

'What do you mean, what's the matter?'

'So nothing's the matter.'

'Nothing particularly.'

'That's all right then. If you didn't rustle your paper so much I could concentrate better, and we could get to sleep sooner.'

'Sorry.'

After a bit he let the paper drop on to the carpet beside the bed, and lay on his back staring, with some ostentation, at the ceiling.

'Don't you want to read any more?'

'Not particularly.'

'I suppose I could go over this on the tube in the morning.'

'It's only a rehearsal, isn't it?'

41

'I know it's "only a rehearsal", but I can't get any real work done on the character if I have to keep shouting "line" to the ASM all the time, can I?'

After she put out the light she lay on her back too, waiting for him to turn to her, as he often did, or at least to hold her hand, as he almost always did. But he didn't move, so she turned on her side, away from him. She waited nevertheless for the rhythm of his breathing to slow into sleep, but it didn't do so. She turned back to him again.

'Something really is the matter, isn't it?'

'It's nothing important.'

'Then there's no reason not to tell me.'

'Promise me you won't be cross.'

'I won't be cross.'

'I wish you'd told me about that scene.'

'What scene?'

'The bedroom scene.'

'You weren't shocked, surely?'

'Of course not. It's just that you never mentioned it.'

'It never struck me that there was anything to mention.'

'So being naked in bed with some other man you hardly know is just part of the day's work?'

'Of course it is, if the play demands it. Anyway, I wasn't completely naked, if that's what's worrying you. I had something on under the bedclothes, and so did he. I thought they shot it quite discreetly. They're very careful on television these days, even if it's something that's going out after nine o'clock.'

He watched the faint gleam of light on the ceiling from the street-lamp outside, but said nothing.

'Actually it isn't true that I hardly know him. We were in the same company when I was at Bristol. He was very sweet about everything. He certainly isn't interested in me in that sort of way. I'm not sure he's interested in women at all.'

'Typical.'

'What do you mean, typical?'

'I mean it's typical of acting altogether – the way the audience just sits there, conned into getting steamed up by a couple in bed who literally couldn't care a fuck for each other.'

'I suppose you'd rather we really fucked each other.'

'Of course I wouldn't.'

'Well then.'

'What do you mean, well then?'

'I don't see what you're objecting to.'

She turned away from him and lay on her back. He shifted his position slightly. A late car drove up in the street below. They listened to the sound of its door slamming, and the retreating footsteps of its owner.

'I just don't like seeing you in bed with another man,' he began again, 'whatever the circumstances.'

'But you're not "in bed" like that with someone when you're on the set with a dozen studio people standing round, lights all over the place, and with make-up redoing your hair for each take. I don't know why you live with an actress if you don't understand the first thing about acting. You're talking about something that wasn't real.'

'You made it feel real. You were very good.'

'All right, it's real in a way. All the same, you always know while you're doing it that you're faking it.'

'It seems rather a pointless way of spending one's life.'

'Please don't be so stuffy about it, darling. It's not that different from the way you spend yours. When you're with your clients or your secretary or at a board meeting you're not the same as you are with me. You're in a role. Everyone performs, most of the time, only they don't realize it.'

'I suppose so,' he conceded, after a pause. 'But in that case what's left that is real? Being in bed together, like we are now, feels extremely real to me. I don't want to share it with millions of other people just because they happen to turn on the television.'

'What you really mean is you don't want to share me. You want my body to belong to you. It doesn't — it's mine. I can't help it if I have to use it for my work, like almost everyone else. Don't be possessive.'

43

'But it's us I'm possessive about – not just you. I don't want an imitation of our intimate life up there on the screen for everybody to gawp at.'

'It wasn't in the least like us. You never crossed my mind.'

'Great. The biggest love scene of your career, and you don't even think of me. Most encouraging.'

He was so unreasonable that she knew he was genuinely hurt. She turned towards him again, and took his hand between hers.

'You're so stupid,' she said tenderly, 'but just think. You know there's a difference between looking and touching. You didn't mind my wearing only the bottom half of my bikini when we were in Corsica, and I didn't mind you staring at all the other topless girls on the beach, behind your sunglasses. I would have minded if you'd started groping them, but you didn't.'

He turned to her, and for the first time in their conversation looked into her eyes, as best he could in the dim light.

'That was only because none of them was as nice as you.'

She squeezed his hand.

'But you let him touch you, while the rest of us were looking.'

'Don't start again, darling. It wasn't my fault. I couldn't help it. It was the way the scene was written. Tell me if you still think I'm nice.'

'Of course I do. I'm sorry. It's just that seeing you like that made me want you – and then I thought of all the other men who must have felt the same, and it upset me.'

'But they're not here with me now, and I don't love them – I love you.'

He was about to reply when they heard a door open and close in the flat above. They lay there listening, until the house quietened once more. She waited, knowing there was still something on his mind.

'I wish we slept like that.'

'Like what?'

'Naked. It made me feel somehow resentful that we don't.'

'But people always do in that sort of scene. It's just a convention

44

– I hadn't thought about it. I suppose it's to make it more exciting.'

'I don't see why the excitement should be kept for them.'

'Why didn't you say?'

'I don't know. I didn't like to suggest it – I kept hoping you would. Anyway, I thought you might get cold.'

'I think you're the silliest man I've ever known,' she said, with yet more softness than before, 'and the sweetest.'

She sat up, took off her nightdress, and threw it aside on the floor. Then, leaning over him, she undid his pyjama buttons, and pressed her breast to his, as she had seemed to do in the play.

'There. Is that better?'

'It's very nice,' he said, a little grudgingly.

'You mustn't get upset about nothing.'

She kissed his brow, his eyelids, his cheek, and ran her forefinger down his nose and along his shut mouth. He didn't part his lips to suck it as he often did, as if he was not, even now, quite placated. Nevertheless, he let her caresses lead to their usual conclusion, after a while.

[3]

DOWN FOR THE DAY

It was remarkable, really, how amicable everything had turned out to be, so far. Robert examined himself briefly in the mirror of the downstairs cloakroom as he washed his hands, trying to remember whether he looked different four – or was it five – years ago.

He had arrived an hour earlier for Sunday morning coffee, after driving down the motorway. Miriam had kissed his cheek very sweetly, and Anthony had shaken his hand with a warmth that seemed completely genuine and which Robert didn't doubt was so.

The house was as elegant as he'd expected it be. Anthony had made money as a publisher and had had money of his own in the first place, and the interiors showed that Miriam hadn't needed to consult anything except her own excellent if conservative taste. Their decision to move to the small Wiltshire town (from which Anthony commuted) became entirely understandable. As they said, it offered so much more in terms of quality of life than London as it had now become. The Georgian rectory they'd bought backed on to the churchyard and, despite being in the town centre, it had a garden as large as one could want or manage. There would be plenty of room for the children to play, as they got older.

49

Before lunch they walked round the flowerbeds and inspected the old-fashioned roses Miriam had decided to go in for.

'This one's particularly lovely, don't you think? The pink is so soft, and it fades so beautifully. The rain spoils it, though.'

'What's it called?'

'Souvenir de la Malmaison. There used to be one in front of the house next door to my old flat. I've always wanted to grow it myself. Do you remember it?'

'I think I was usually in too much of a hurry to notice.'

She turned away to rescue a haughty Burmese cat which one of the toddlers was clumsily trying to embrace.

Lunch lasted well into the afternoon. They got through a bottle of quite serious claret without difficulty, even though Miriam as always drank little. Afterwards they sat about, desultorily turning over the Sunday papers. Robert, a literary journalist who also did arts features for television, wrote for one of them; he and Anthony had a good deal in common. He gave them a rather worked-up account of what really happened when he'd tried to film an interview with a South American novelist of great reputation and baffling incoherence. They seemed amused.

Eventually the two men decided they ought to walk off their meal. As it was Sunday there wasn't much traffic. Anthony pointed out some good buildings whose façades hadn't yet been ruined by chain stores or savings banks. 'But much the best thing is the parish church,' he said. 'There's something in it I'd like to show you.'

Robert hadn't been inside a church for a long time. 'Do you actually come to services here?' he asked, trying to keep the incredulity out of his voice.

'Yes, we do. Miriam specially likes evensong. We began to take to it after we moved – we never used to go. The choir isn't up to cathedral standards of course, but it's good. Look, this is what I wanted you to see.'

The medieval couple rested stiffly on top of their tomb, the knight clad in armour but with his ankles almost skittishly crossed, his lady holding a nosegay, to ward off plague perhaps. They seemed

50

to feel that because they were lying together in public they had to maintain expressions of stony propriety, even in effigy.

'I like the little dog at their feet, don't you?' said Anthony. 'I wonder what it was called.'

'What about Trey, or Blanch, or Sweetheart,' suggested Robert, remembering his *Lear*.

Robert enjoyed their walk. Anthony was easy to get on with, and he didn't appear to be put out by the past in any way. Either he didn't really know much about it, or didn't mind, or had got over it, or had simply been too busy to think about it. One could never tell, in such situations.

Light summer rain began to drift across the garden as they got back, and instead of the promised tea on the lawn they had it in the drawing-room. To make it more cheery, and despite the season, Miriam put a match to the carefully arranged logs in the period grate. After tea and anchovy toast, Robert – whose Sundays were usually solitary and who often preferred to work that day – started to flag. Exhausted by the effort, and the embarrassment, of reading a story to the three year old about a policeman and a grasshopper, he fell into a doze.

He woke abruptly because the phone was ringing, and became aware that Miriam – sitting in a low chair opposite him with some needlework – had been watching him. She didn't turn away as he struggled to shake off his torpor. As she began to say, 'It's all right, Anthony will take it in the study,' they could hear him doing so through the half-open doors across the hall.

'I'm so sorry,' said Robert, 'I must have dropped off. Not used to such a good lunch.'

'Don't apologize. I like people to feel at home. Besides,' she added, 'I always liked to look at you asleep.'

Anthony put down the phone in the other room and came in, his earlier equanimity clearly upset.

'Darling, that was Sam. I was going to have a meeting with him tomorrow afternoon, but now he's got to fly to Frankfurt in the morning, so I'll have to talk to him over breakfast.'

'But that means you'll have to go back to town tonight.'

'I know – it's a real pain, but I do have to see him.'

'I really ought to be pushing off myself,' said Robert, feeling distinctly in the way, and also suddenly envious of the domestic tranquillity that had been disturbed. 'I could easily give you a lift.'

'My dear chap, there's no need for you to go. Why don't you stay and keep Miriam company for a bit? I'm just sorry I have to rush off – there isn't a late train on Sundays.'

By the time Miriam had got her husband's things together, driven him round to the station in her car, and put the little ones to bed, Robert had had a good hour to himself. He put some more wood on the gently smoking fire although there was now a low watery sun outside, poured himself a drink he didn't really want, and began to dip into a new title from Anthony's list. Although the house could hardly be more comfortable he wasn't at ease, and felt homesick for his disorderly flat. It was partly because he was an intruder here, but mostly because memories, never fully quelled anyway, were now yet further from being stilled.

In fact, they had never lost touch, despite the tensions of the break-up. They had a respect as well as a residual concern for each other that stifled recrimination. They went on meeting socially, a situation made less tense when Miriam unexpectedly announced her decision to marry Anthony. Robert had seen them less since their move, but they kept promising to ask him down for the day, and here at last he was.

'What would you like to eat?' asked Miriam, finally free from the bedtime rituals on which the children insisted.

'Nothing much. I'm not really hungry. An omelette perhaps – some cheese – anything.'

They had their supper cosily, on a trolley near the fire.

'Your omelettes were always so much better than anyone else's.'

'You can get such good free-range eggs round here.'

The summer dusk deepened. Miriam drew the curtains. They sat on the sofa and watched the flicker of a flame as it crept along a log which had a twist of ivy-stem clinging to it.

'Not quite "Frost at Midnight",' said Miriam.

'Don't be pretentious,' said Robert. 'I bet you haven't read the poem since you were a student, and probably not even then.'

She looked pleased as he reverted to an old tone, and then her smile relaxed into seriousness, as their mutual gaze continued.

'Are you happy?' he said. 'You look wonderful.'

'Yes,' she said, 'yes, I am happy, I think – as happy as one is likely to be, in the long run. You look wonderful too – not a day older.'

'People keep telling me how well I am. When I'm finally laid on the slab they'll crowd round and say doesn't he look fit.'

After a pause he asked, 'How is your writing going?'

'It isn't. No time – and no inclination either. I never had the talent you thought I had.'

'I don't believe that.'

'I don't read as much as I did. It's partly the children, I suppose. Would you like to look at television?' she said, after another pause.

'Not particularly. I know it's part of my living, but I don't like it. It's not real to me.'

'Would you like some more coffee?'

'Not specially.'

Miriam touched the back of his left hand, as it lay on the sofa between them, with the fingers of her right. 'And what about you? Have you been happy? I've often wanted to ask, but there were always people around, and you're so different then. There must have been others, since me.'

'One or two – well, two or three – but they didn't stay. I can't blame them. I just wasn't there. I've been all right,' he added, anxious not to seem self-pitying.

She looked touched nevertheless. 'Was it bad when I left?'

'Yes, it was.' He wondered whether to tell her how ill he'd felt after trying to drown his sorrows in Scotch, how he'd walked out of a cinema during a love scene because it brought her nakedness back to him so unbearably, how often he'd walked miles through the evening streets so as to tire himself and his mind out. 'It was very bad. While it lasted.'

He turned to her, and was amazed to see that her eyes were beginning to glisten. She moved closer to him, so that there was no space between them, and rested her face gently on his shoulder, as she used to do.

'Poor Robert,' she said.

He put his arm round her almost automatically and stroked her hair, looking over her head at the now ashen fire. The house was so quiet that he could hear nothing but her breathing; its rhythm was just as he remembered it. Her eyes were shut and she might almost have been asleep, except for the occasional stir of her body as it pressed yet more softly on him. He said nothing; there was no need to say anything; there was nothing to say. He felt sure that if he wanted to they could lie together, as before, that if he asked her she would take him in, as before. She sighed lightly; perhaps she really was asleep now. He acknowledged that he still loved her, that he had never stopped loving her, that he would never not love her, but he felt at rest, for the moment. He wished that the two of them could slowly petrify, as night and silence thickened, so as to be at rest for good.

OLD FRIENDS

When he woke up, in the middle of the afternoon, she was still there beside him, her breathing, as she slept, as light as it had always been. They only had a sheet over them because it was unusually hot for early summer. He drew it back gently and looked at her nakedness in the curtained light. How had he lived without that for so long? He turned to lie on his back, but the movement disturbed her. She raised herself on one elbow to look down at him, and traced his eyebrows with her middle finger, as she used to do.

'So it's really you,' she said, smiling.

'It's me all right,' he said, as he pulled her on to him.

Alan and Joanna had met, quite by chance, in the street. She was getting out of her just-parked car when he pulled up in the space behind. For a long moment they had simply stood, wryly conceding through their held gaze that they were glad – overjoyed, even – to see each other, despite what had passed. 'How are *you*?' they'd both said, almost simultaneously. They embraced in some confusion – he tried to kiss her on the cheek while she ducked in order to give him a big hug – but they laughed it off happily.

'What are you doing round here?'

'I live round here. What are you doing?'

'Oh, just shopping. Nothing special.'

'In that case, why don't we have a drink?'

'Why don't we – it's such a nice day.'

They soon fell back into their old comfortable tones. It began to seem no time at all since they last met. She'd got married six months after they'd split up, but he'd never known whether her feelings about the man who was now her husband were the cause or the consequence of their separation. She was on her own for the moment because Charles was abroad, at a conference.

'Why didn't you go with him? Nothing wrong with a few days in Florence at this time of year.'

'I don't know. I didn't feel like it, somehow. There are things I want to do at home.'

'What things?'

'Oh, this and that. I felt like a little time to myself – just for a change, you know.'

She stared out of the pub window at a tired woman behind a pushchair with a sleeping baby slumped in it, a sun-hat tipped over its face at a rakish angle. They were waiting to cross the busy road.

'I don't mean that we're not happy,' she said. 'Everything's fine. I can't wait for him to get back.'

She looked at him with that air of tender concern which was so familiar, although he'd never been sure how genuine it was, or how lasting.

'And how are you, really?'

He knew that what she actually wanted to know was who her current successor was, and what she was like. Alan replied rather stiffly that his girlfriend was also away, looking after her mother during her annual week by the sea. What was her name? Names were important to Joanna; she felt they told her a lot. Her name was Angie. Joanna's reaction was non-committal, as if with a name like that one had to reserve judgement.

'Since we're both obviously free,' he said, 'I can't see any reason why we shouldn't have lunch together.'

'Nor can I,' she said, taking his arm.

They laughed a good deal over lunch – more than they used to, Alan thought. He couldn't but remember how much in love with her he'd been, but he had to some extent forgotten how much he enjoyed her company, most of the time. He felt increasingly exhilarated as the meal went on, partly because he ordered better wine than he could normally afford. Joanna didn't notice this extravagance; she had clearly got used to having more money than in the old days. It struck him that her clothes must have been expensive. Charles was presumably well-off. Alan wondered briefly if that was what she married him for, and then felt ashamed of thinking in such a way of a woman who had given up a lot for him, one way and another, in the past.

'I know this sounds a bit ridiculous,' he said, 'but would you like to come back to my place for coffee? You haven't seen my new flat.'

She looked touched, even indulgent.

'I don't see why not,' she said, with the ironically rueful smile that had always entranced him. 'After all, we're old friends.'

They left their cars where they were, to be picked up later, and made their way through the bright streets, pausing to look at desirable objects in shop windows as they used to, finding themselves holding hands as they once did. Joanna wasn't put off by prices that still seemed prohibitive to Alan. 'Tell me about your house,' he said. 'I suppose it's full of nice pieces. Couldn't I come round some time?'

'I don't think that would be a good idea. It's belonged to Charles for ages, even before his first marriage. How far is it now?'

Fortunately the flat didn't look too untidy when they arrived. It had become much better organized since Angie had moved in. She liked to put things away – so much so, in fact, that he couldn't find the coffee-pot, and called Joanna in to help him. The kitchen was narrow – hardly more than a galley – and as he straightened up after exploring a low shelf she was so close that he couldn't stop himself putting his arms round her. Miraculously, she didn't object, but gently pressed herself against him in return. He closed his eyes.

'I feel dizzy,' he said.

'It's the heat, and all that wine,' she said. 'Perhaps you should lie down.'

They watched each other undress from opposite sides of the bed; it was a habit they'd got into early on. What followed was for him simpler, and easier, and more wonderful than it had ever been. Later, as she started to pick up her clothes from the floor, he tried to detain her.

'Can't you stay a bit longer? Don't dress again so soon. You know how I love to see you like that.'

She gave him a brief smile but disappeared into the bathroom all the same, frowning a little to herself as she went. When she emerged she was ready for the street once more. After drawing back the curtains, she came over to the bed where he was still lying. She sat down on its edge, and took his hand.

'It was lovely to see you,' she said. 'Promise me you'll take care of yourself.'

'When can I see you again? Can I see you again soon?'

She put her finger to his lips, as if shushing a child.

'It's best to leave it.'

'I don't want to leave it. I don't want you to leave me, now you've come back.'

'I haven't come back, and I'm not going to. And anyway, what about Angie?'

'Angie?' For a second Alan couldn't think who she meant. 'That doesn't matter.'

'Well, it should. I do care about you, but you must realize that I couldn't go through all that again.'

She bent over him, kissed his forehead, and was gone before he could protest further.

After lying on his back for what seemed a long time he turned over, his face in the pillow which still smelt slightly of her perfume. He would have liked to cry – it would have been fitting – but no tears came. He lay on his side and stared at the digits on the clock-radio, surprised that it wasn't as late as he'd thought. The sun was lower, but still strong. It threw a shadow from an upright chair in front of the window. He waited for the shadow to move, and found that after a while it had done so without his noticing. He had no idea what to do.

After a shower he put on some clean clothes, and made the cup of tea she wouldn't stay for. He opened the window wider, moved the chair near it, and sat down with a book. After an hour he had read only five pages. The noise from the street below made it hard to concentrate, but he kept the window open because he liked to feel the warm air.

Would it continue fine? He turned on the television to catch the forecast. Yes, it seemed so, particularly in the south-west. Angie and her mother were being lucky with the weather.

Alan made himself think about Angie, admitting with some mortification that for much of the time he didn't do so. He liked having her around; he enjoyed her company, and physically she was sufficiently responsive. She appeared to like being with him, but she was neither demonstrative nor demanding. All the same, she had a claim, and one which he hadn't done much to honour.

One of Angie's many advantages was that she didn't probe. For her, the past was the past, as far as he could tell. Alan was sure, for instance, that she'd never searched his desk when he was out, which was just as well: the bottom left-hand drawer housed a cache of Joanna's letters which might have disturbed even Angie's equanimity. Alan tried to decide whether to open the drawer himself – something he hadn't thought of doing, or hadn't dared to do, for a long time. Eventually he went across to the desk, squatted in front of it, and pulled out an envelope at random. 'The flat. Tuesday. Darling Alan, I know this will hurt you, but I've got to say it . . .' There was no need for him to read on. It came back to him like something he'd been forced to learn by heart long ago. Thinking of the wounded and wounding words he'd sent in reply, he put the letter back and shut the drawer.

He went over to the window again, and looked out. The lights had come on too early for so bright an evening. He ought to collect the car and get something to eat; better make the bed first, though. As he straightened the sheets and replaced the cover, he began to sense a tremor within. He knelt by the bed, and rested his forehead on its side. He looked as if he might be praying, but he wasn't.

After ten or fifteen minutes he went to the bathroom, pressed a cold flannel to his face, put on his jacket, and left the house. The air outside was soft, almost aromatic, as if it was in the south. He put out his hand to a lamp-post, for support, before setting off.

When he got to the car it looked different somehow. He even wondered if it was really his, but it opened to his key. His gloves, maps, and cassettes were all there. He sat behind the wheel for some time, wondering where to go.

Once clear of the city, the motorway was quiet, now that night had fallen. He kept his speed down and stayed in the nearside lane, letting others − confident of their destination − sweep past him. The pressure of his foot on the throttle was so light that the car seemed to move through its own momentum. It embarrassed him to think that 'driving into the night' was something that his younger self would have found romantic. The laconic hero of some *film noir*, trilby pulled down, face in half-shadow, he drew on the cigarette in the corner of his mouth, the back-projected signs of bars and hotels passing behind him like lighthouses. He would have known where he was going.

Alan was in flight, not pursuit. He couldn't face going back to the flat because it would be too full of Joanna's recent presence, and therefore of her future absence. Nevertheless he couldn't help dwelling not only on today's encounter but on earlier scenes, dialogues, and intimacies which replayed themselves over and over again in his mind. Long-suppressed images − of Joanna asleep, in the bath, cooking, looking up at him from her book, waiting for him at the bus-stop − kept forming themselves on the windscreen and coming between him and the dark road.

He tried to visualize Angie instead. He realized for the first time – consciously at any rate – that the motorway would take him almost as far as the small resort where she and her mother were staying. He could give them a surprise visit. Angie would like that; she was not so placid as not to enjoy the unexpected. He'd never met her mother, so he couldn't tell how she would react if he suddenly appeared for breakfast.

The woods and fields at the side of the road that had been drifting by for he didn't know how long were abruptly replaced for a few miles by low cliffs of bare chalk. They shone with disconcerting whiteness under the headlights. It was a gorge cut through the top of the downs. Alan recalled that soon after this there was a service area. He'd better get some petrol while he could.

At this time of night the café was almost deserted. Two lorry-drivers stirred their tea apathetically while a motor-cyclist, swinging his crash-helmet by its chin-strap, tried to chat up the waitress. She looked bored. Alan thought how strange it must be to work here, in the middle of nowhere. He drank some milk out of a carton, and ate a damp ham sandwich.

Although he still felt shaky, he was glad to get back to his car, and on the road again. From time to time unpredictable vapours began to roll towards him, engulfing him, so that he momentarily lost his bearings. He'd always hated driving in fog. He was in the middle of one patch of mist, straining to keep the cat's-eyes in view, when he started to talk aloud. If he'd had a car-phone he'd have used it, no matter what the time was. 'It isn't fair,' he said. 'You shouldn't have come back if you were going away again. You always were capricious. How do you expect me to cope now, just when I was getting over it? You don't think what it's like for me. You never did.' By this time he was banging his hand on the steering-wheel, and had to grab it suddenly when there was a scraping noise. He pulled over to the hard shoulder, got out and examined the offside wing. He'd hit the central barrier, but not seriously enough to prevent him driving on. After a while the mists thinned away.

Alan couldn't remember when he'd last seen the dawn, but he didn't appear to have missed much. The new day seemed reluctant

61

to get going, despite the forecast. He left the motorway and passed along deep-cut lanes like tunnels before approaching, at last, the sea. He left the car behind a long embankment of shingle, near some dilapidated huts with tattered curtains, and took the cliff path, following the white-splashed stones that marked its course. Higher up, he could just make out, on the far side of the bay, a few individual houses, rising irregularly behind the harbour. Angie would be asleep in one of them, her arm over her face. The sea was calm and grey in the early light. The sky was grey too, the clouds closely folded on each other, not low, but heavy.

Alan could never make up his mind about the sea. Sometimes he longed for it, and felt that to be near it would bring him peace. At other times he was relieved that, unlike so many others, he didn't have to waste tedious weeks beside it every summer. Still, now he was here, he might as well go down to the water's edge.

The shingle was so deep that crossing it was an effort. The bank shelved steeply, so that you had to allow for slippage with each step. Watching where he put his feet reminded him of something he couldn't place. From this angle the sea looked greener and more purposeful, although he couldn't decide whether the tide was coming in or going out. There was some sort of cargo boat ahead; he wished he'd brought some binoculars. Along the shore to his left stood a pair of anglers, their rods at their feet, looking out to where they hoped the fish were. One of them turned to trudge up the slope, and Alan found what he couldn't remember earlier. It was a picture of Joanna, her body amazingly brown, picking her way fastidiously across a rough Mediterranean beach. The photo must be in his desk somewhere. 'I do wish these rocks weren't so hard on my feet,' she'd said in her rueful way, while he was taking the shot. 'You'd have thought the sea would have smoothed them out a bit, after all this time.' 'Don't be so feeble,' he'd replied, his heart turning over with love, then and now.

He felt a stronger breeze on his face, and tasted the salt on his lips. The rattle of the shingle, as the foam pulled it back, had got louder. He was so tired that climbing back seemed beyond him.

The water filled his shoes with the first step. It was cold, but the sensation wasn't unpleasant. By the time it had risen to his thighs, stone had given way to sand, which made his footing firmer. You had to take one step at a time and pick your moment, in the troughs. At first he braced himself against the waves, but as he got deeper he learned to ride rather than resist them; it was as if you had to let the sea roll through you. Even so, with the water at chest-height, it became harder to remain steady. By spreading out his arms he was able to keep his balance well enough to twist his head and look round. The fishermen were moving slowly towards him, impeded by their heavy boots as well as the sliding shingle. He faced the sea again, and forced his body forward. As he did so, the land beneath him fell away, and the water took his weight.

[4]

THE BRIDGE

On the evening of the day his wife finally left him Richard celebrated by making love to another woman. That was not, of course, quite how he put it to himself. Nevertheless, he felt a strong urge to mark the day of his release from a situation which had long been deteriorating, and a declaration of sexual independence seemed the appropriate way to do it. He had resisted temptation so far and much good it had done him. What was there for him to be loyal to now?

Julia had announced her departure at breakfast, a time of day when she was normally full of businesslike energy and when Richard was not at his best – one of their many small incompatibilities.

'I think I should tell you, Richard, that I'm leaving today. I don't want to leave a note, or anything like that.'

'What do you mean, leaving? When will you be back?'

'Well, I'll be back to collect some more of my stuff, and we can talk about which things you want and which I'd like to have. There's no hurry. I'll give you a ring.'

'You mean you're *not* coming back?'

'Richard, I do wish you weren't so slow in the mornings. Why you try to read the paper at this time of day I can't think – you never take any of it in. I'm leaving today because I'm moving in with Peter.'

Although he had long anticipated what was happening, Richard didn't say anything because, now that it was real, he felt too ill to do so. Julia, with the intuitive perception of the married, realized this, and was touched.

'You'll be all right, darling. It's for the best, really it is.'

He saw that her eyes had that shine they always had when she was close to tears. She rose from the table, kissed the top of his head as she passed, and said, as she went out of the room, 'You know we don't love each other any more, not as we should, not as we did.'

Richard turned round and was about to reply, but by then she was already upstairs, collecting her bits and pieces. He didn't move from the kitchen. Shortly afterwards the front door opened and then shut again.

Fortunately his day at the office wasn't too strenuous. One of the firm's more demanding authors had to be given a less expensive lunch than he felt was his due, but Richard's amiability in such situations was so practised that by the end of the meal his guest had become quite docile. During the afternoon Richard tried to make some headway with a manuscript on which a decision was needed, but after a couple of hours at it he found he had little idea of its contents, let alone its merits. Best to leave it till the weekend perhaps, and take it home. At least it would be quiet there now.

About tea-time one of the newer editors rang to ask if she could see him on a matter trivial enough for it to be obvious that it was a pretext. When she came in they smiled at each other uncertainly. After a pause, Richard said, 'Sue, I've been meaning to thank you for coming to Brighton with me, for that presentation. I'm afraid I talked too much afterwards, though I can't remember what I said. Sorry about that.'

'That's all right. It wasn't the first time a man has told me the story of his life in a bar. Perhaps some of it was true. I enjoyed it, anyway.'

'I'm not sure what the truth is any more. By the way, are you staying for drinks tonight? It won't last too long. We might go on somewhere afterwards, if you'd like to.'

She looked straight at him for a moment.

'All right,' she said.

The office party wasn't the conventional Christmas saturnalia – it was the wrong season – but a decorous send-off for a retiring director. As a recently elected member of the Board Richard had to be there, but he steered Sue away as soon as he decently could. During dinner they mostly gossiped about professional matters, and it was not until they'd reached the sorbet that Richard said, after looking round the restaurant as if to be sure no one was there whom he knew, 'I'm sorry if I seem a bit subdued. The fact is that my wife walked out this morning – not dramatically, you understand – we'd both been expecting it for some time.'

Sue put her hand over his, on the tablecloth.

After his confession Richard felt increasingly relaxed. It was a great relief to be with a woman who as far as he was concerned had no history, but who appeared to find him agreeable.

As they walked away she took his arm and said, with light irony, 'Perhaps this is the point at which one of us is supposed to say, My place or yours?'

Richard thought of his empty house, the breakfast things still on the table, the unmade bed. 'Oh, yours, I think,' he said, equally lightly, 'don't you?'

Her flat was some distance away, not far from the river. In the taxi they kissed each other speculatively. Inside, her room was unexpectedly warm. 'I can't bear coming back to a cold place,' she said, 'especially when one lives alone – at least, most of the time,' she added, with a certain archness. Richard let the implication drift past. He liked being with Sue and was beginning to desire her, but he could not pretend an interest in her private life, not at this stage.

They sat on the sofa together while they had some more coffee, and began to kiss again.

'I must leave you for a moment,' she said.

When she returned she waited just inside the room, naked to the waist, holding the door-handle. He stood as she came up to him, so that he could touch first one breast, and then the other, with his fingertips. Their breathing quickened; she took off the rest of her clothes and began to undress him; they fell to the carpet. Richard knew that his need for the imminent release was uncontainable, and that it would not bring him what he wanted. He cried out, and then continued to sob, before quietening gradually. 'Was it so wonderful for you?' she asked. He buried his face more deeply in her neck. 'I'm glad it was,' she said. 'Don't move. I love your weight on me.' After a bit he turned his head the other way. At floor-level he could see some fluffy slippers pushed under a chair. Looking up, he realized that a portable television set on a small table had been casting its pale eye over the proceedings.

He disengaged himself with the usual slight embarrassment while also attempting the tenderness he felt was the least he could show.

'It's very late. You must get some sleep.'

'You can stay here, if you like.'

'That's sweet of you, but I have to go home for some things I'll need in the morning.'

'Well, it's nice to know that I'll see you in the morning. At the office,' she added, seeing that he looked vague.

'Yes, of course. At the office,' he said, and kissed her lightly on the cheek before he went.

The night air felt raw, as it does in London. Richard set off from the flat, not thinking much about his direction, and soon found himself at the Embankment. Not many people about now, but vehicles, released in batches by the lights, still slid along the wide road beside the river. He crossed it, and leaned on the stone parapet. He suddenly felt so tired he could hardly move, and let himself slump over it. A car drew up, and two uniformed men got out.

'Are you all right, sir?' said one of them, with the studied

70

politeness of a man expecting, but scrupulously not wanting to anticipate, a drunken reply.

'I'm fine, officer, thank you,' said Richard, trying to appear urbane. 'Just a little faint, that's all.'

'Live near here, do you, sir?'

'Not far,' said Richard, moving off, 'not far.'

The police returned reluctantly to their car – slightly piqued, Richard felt, at his apparent sobriety – and drove away.

He walked slowly, and then more slowly, along the pavement, from one street-lamp to the next, until he came to the iron bridge. His feet began to hurt but, although it was dry, he could hardly take his shoes off. He began to cross the bridge and looked down at the river, black as the tarmac in parallel with it. Which way was the tide going? Hard to tell. What had happened that evening seemed further away now than his breakfast conversation with his wife. He tried to recall what it was like when he first made love to her, but it was a blank, as if the recent scene had automatically erased all its predecessors. But when he was half-way across and had begun to think about what to do in the morning, his memory cleared. It came back to him completely – the place, the time, all the little details he thought he'd lost for ever.

'Don't go,' he shouted, as if to someone on the opposite bank. 'Don't go,' he cried again, gripping the bridge's iron railing as if his life depended on it.

THE STATUE AND THE BUST

They met once a month, usually in a restaurant for lunch, sometimes in a pub after work, according to what could be arranged. In the early days he found the intervals between hard to bear, and the short time they allowed themselves to spend together was too intense, too packed with half-suppressed emotion to be pleasurable. Their story was that they were old friends, used to work in the same office; there was no reason (happily married as they both were) why they shouldn't keep in touch. In practice, they sought out eating-places that were a bit off the map, so that they were never spotted by mutual acquaintances. 'I wish it didn't feel quite so like *Brief Encounter*,' she said. He pointed out that at least they weren't condemned to meet at railway stations. But they gradually became less nervous as other preoccupations and responsibilities supervened – both were keen not to let their promising careers estrange them from their families – and as they became resigned to the idea that their physical desire for each other was not going to be fulfilled.

At first, he would eagerly note what she was wearing, how she looked – whether thinner or fuller in the body of which he was so conscious, under her clothes, that his hand holding the wine glass would tremble until he'd had enough drink to calm him. She understood this, and began to dress more soberly. Initially, they got through a bottle at a sitting; later, a glass each was enough. For the first year or so they talked almost exclusively of what they had been feeling about each other since they last met, each wanting to know when the other's sense of separation had been most acute. They clutched at the straws of memory provided by the times – few enough – when they had been together, when things, trivial in themselves, had happened to them alone. But this self-absorption gave way in time to enquiries of a more dispassionate kind; they exchanged amiable sentiments about their respective spouses, and monitored the progress of their various children with parental fellow-feeling. At the same time it remained clear to both of them that they were meeting as lovers rather than friends. Neither of them ever proposed introducing the other at home, nor did either ever speak of the other there. They kept to the vow they had made on – of all places – a channel ferry.

She was already well established in the firm when he joined. She was thought to offer an excellent role-model as a professional woman in her early thirties who had had her children early, and was now entitled to feel serene about how self-sufficient they were, for their ages. They knew Mummy's work was important to her, and in their juvenile way they backed her up. She was so used to the feeling of her life being under control that his intrusion into her consciousness was a shock. She hadn't expected *all that* to happen, to her. So when she found herself timing her visits to the photocopier so that they coincided with his or lying in wait for him in the corridor at the end of the day, she was dismayed. When he said one evening, 'Have you time for a quick drink?' she had felt so breathless that she could only nod her assent.

After that first meeting – by unspoken agreement they made for a wine bar some distance from the office – they rationed themselves to an hour or two a week, always in some semi-public place. It wasn't long before they acknowledged their desire for each other, but they both felt strongly that they should at least defer its consummation. They were old enough – and, they told each other, wise enough – to know that there are some frontiers one should be very careful

74

about crossing for fear of not being able to get back again, and that once they had been to bed together they would be in another country. The structure of their separate lives was each in its way satisfactory and shouldn't be destabilized for what was probably a temporary intoxication. And of course it wouldn't be right to wound those to whom they were bound. It seemed best for him to change his job, which he was able to do without disadvantage.

They continued to endorse these high-minded resolves for some months, looking deeply into each other's eyes as they did so in a way which was hardly in the spirit of what they were saying, holding each other at parting with anguish. Then an entirely unexpected combination of events pushed them together. She was on holiday with the family on the continent when he too was sent abroad to placate an important client. On the return journey he drifted into the bar on the channel ferry (it was one of the longer crossings) and was astonished to see her sitting alone, reading a newspaper over a gin. She had had to leave for home prematurely, leaving the others to follow on, because of the sudden – though as it turned out not critical – illness of her mother. It must be fate, they said, with an irony in which they did not quite believe. They realized that they now had several hours in which they were, in effect, on their own. They wandered about on deck in the restless way ferry passengers do, looking for niches behind lifeboats and bulkheads where they could discreetly embrace. He was entranced by the way the wind blew her hair back from her unlined forehead.

They began to consider whether they should look for an empty cabin. They would have to ask someone for a key, and pay extra – not that that mattered. 'But I know what would happen,' she said. 'We wouldn't be able to stop ourselves making love on one of those narrow bunks. It's against everything we've said.' 'Yes,' he said, stroking her hair, 'that's what would happen – that's what I want to happen, but I agree it shouldn't happen.' There was the further problem that neither of them was, contraceptively speaking, prepared for the coincidence of their meeting; they could hardly ask the steward. 'It's all right,' he said. 'Don't worry. I've thought of what it would be like so much – been through it in my head so often – that I don't mind taking the wish for the deed.' 'I love you even more for being so good to me,' she said. They clung hard to each other, as if to make the clothes between them melt. They vowed to remain in love with each other for the rest of their lives, hoping to appease frustration by fidelity. As they went their respective and disconsolate ways, back in England, they tried to feel pleased with themselves for having resisted opportunity.

Nevertheless, their first few meetings after this episode were tense with revivified desire. They both continued to imagine the scene they had hung back from playing. They knew how it would go, up to its climax, and would often re-run it in their minds. At the same time, they could not be confident about its aftermath. She was frightened that his love would become either more demanding or less so, according to whether the gift of her body surpassed or disappointed his expectations. He was apprehensive about their becoming committed to a career of adultery – he flinched internally at the word – with all its degrading deceits.

One day, as they were sitting in his car after one of their semi-clandestine lunches, she said, 'I think we ought to face the fact that we don't, really, want it enough. Otherwise it would have happened. We're like the lovers in Browning's poem who let their desire cool until their own bodies were replaced by a statue and a bust. Browning disapproved of course.' 'I hate Browning,' he said, 'all that optimism.' 'I agree. He seemed to think that all you had to do was to do what you had to do, and to hell with other people,' she said, dimly remembering an essay she had once written and doing perhaps less than justice to the poet's position. 'I've simply got to get back,' he said, 'because I mustn't be late home – children's birthday party.' 'Poor you. I'll think of you. I still do, all the time. Sometimes I wonder if it's better this way because I feel surer of loving you longer.' They kissed goodbye with passionate chasteness.

She would usually ring him at work to fix their next meeting, but after the customary month she hadn't called. He was concerned, but not greatly. Perhaps there was some domestic problem, or maybe she thought it best to miss a meeting to help things cool down. But when after a further four weeks he still hadn't heard from her he began to be anxious. He couldn't seriously believe that – after all their promises – she meant to break off their relationship, but he feared it all the same. She wasn't, surely, that sort of person – yet who knows what sort of person a person is, when it comes to a certain point? He told himself that he trusted her love, but would understand if, through conscience or fatigue, she had decided that she had had enough.

He learned what had actually happened through a chance conversation with a colleague of hers at some professional get-together. After bringing their desultory gossip round to her in an elaborately casual way, he was told that there was bad news. 'She's been away for some weeks – some form of cancer, I gather. Obviously we all hope they've caught it in time. There are young children, you know.'

After murmuring a few appropriate phrases he pretended to remember that he had to make a phone-call, and got out into the street as quickly as possible. He walked fast for some time without any thought of direction. Out of breath, he leaned face foremost against a solid iron double-door, resting his forehead on the cool black metal, and tried not to sob. 'You all right, mate?' said a voice behind him. 'Fine,' he replied, 'I'm fine,' and turned away.

There was no point in panic, however, until he knew the exact truth about her condition. Because of their habitual secrecy they had no mutual friends, but by going through in his mind all those he used to know in the offices where she still worked he was able to think of two people who might have reliable information. Sustained, to some degree, by the prospect of action – he would ring these contacts in the morning – he slowly made his way home.

When he got in next day he found something on his desk which made everything clear. It was her first, and last, letter to him:

You will be surprised to hear from me in this way. I feel I know how to talk to you, but not how to write to you. I know anyway that you will be sorry to learn that I am seriously ill. It's cancer — I've always been afraid of it, and now I've got it. Everyone is supportive and encouraging, but I know that it's one of the kinds which don't give you very long. The pain keeps getting worse, and I have to increase the drugs. It's hard to think properly in this state, and I find it's easier to cope if I don't think too much about you — forgive me for this, and for everything else. Please don't write or try to see me. I'll probably have to go into the hospice soon anyway. I have loved you, and do love you, but I've got to stop thinking about all that now. Pray for me.

The most difficult thing to do, in the circumstances, was to do nothing. He didn't write, according to her wish, and made no attempt to find out how her condition was developing. As he sat at his desk, he would bite his finger so hard that the marks on his skin took some time to fade. He took to chewing sweets and even gum because otherwise his jaw would clench so tightly that his teeth hurt. When he didn't hear what his wife or children said to him, he would apologize with excessive tenderness. He avoided looking at himself in the mirror as far as possible, fearful that his internal struggle for composure was too evident in his face. The effort to appear unchanged took a great deal out of him, but it was the least he could do for her. The anguish of not seeing her, not comforting her, not holding her, must be as nothing compared with the terminal agonies she was at that moment undergoing. He dared not imagine too closely what was happening to the body he had so wanted to possess.

Fortunately, when the worst came he knew about it almost immediately. Her firm wrote to present and recently past employees to notify them of the date of the funeral, and asking for contributions towards a trust-fund to help with her children's education. The early death of a talented colleague had clearly touched a corporate nerve, and the firm wanted to behave well. He replied in studiously appropriate terms and enclosed a cheque for more than he could really afford, but not so much as to attract notice.

Going to the funeral itself was out of the question, but he felt quite unable to work normally. After frittering away the morning in the most anodyne tasks he could find, he took a long lunch-hour during which he loitered outside the restaurant they had most often been to. He stood on the opposite side of the street watching those who went in and out, and waited until an obviously happy couple emerged, laughing at each other, holding hands, at ease together.

He had to eat something himself, and went to a fast-food place. The bread tasted like sawdust and the coffee was nauseating. Back at the office to collect his things, he rang home to explain that a problem had blown up involving the continental client he'd visited before; someone had to go and sort it out straightaway. He was brilliantly reassuring – of course he'd be all right. He wouldn't need pyjamas on the night boat, and he always carried a toothbrush in his briefcase anyway. Volunteering to go at such short notice was bound to do him good professionally. As usual, his wife was incurious about his work, being preoccupied with children and other matters.

It was difficult to tell if it was the same ferry as before. He hadn't noticed its name, and there was more than one boat of the same type. In any case it was dark this time, and with fewer people the passenger areas looked different. In the bar he sat down at a low table which at least resembled the one they had used, and drank some gin because she had done so. He felt that he was waiting to be told something, so that it was important to stay alert. He diluted the gin with more tonic, wondered whether he could face a meal, found the cafeteria was closed, and crunched his way through a bag of crisps instead.

He got up and – leaving the bar to three or four solitary drinkers already half-asleep over their evening papers – began a patrol of the whole ship. He ended up on the cabin deck, one level above the lower depths where the empty cars and lorries waited, bumper to bumper, manacled to the oily floor with heavy chains.

He found a cabin with its door left open, and went in. The bunks were certainly narrow; there was hardly room for two to lie side by side, except that he would have been lying not just with her but on her. The thought made him stand rigid for at least a minute while he waited for his hands to unclench and his breathing to become less agitated. He lay down on the bunk and stared at the circular air-conditioning vent in the ceiling. Because he was on his back the tears ran slowly across his temples towards his ears, a sensation he could not remember feeling before. He made no attempt to brush them away until a middle-aged couple came in, claiming – politely enough – that this was their cabin; he must have mistaken the number. He stared at them for a moment without saying anything before stumbling over the high threshold into the corridor.

Out on the open deck the rush of air at the bow was too strong. There was more shelter at the stern. The increased smell of oil-fuel, coupled with the steady rumble of the engines below, was not uncomforting. There was no one about.

He realized that he had always hoped that what they had both wanted to happen would happen despite everything, that he had counted on it happening sometime, even after they had agreed – on this spot or on one identical to it – that it should not happen. He looked out at the broad track of the ship's wake; the white foam glistened faintly. Nothing seemed valuable to him except what he had not had. He tried to see below the surface of the water, but it was too dark.

He sat on the rail with his back to the sea and, as he had seen people do when on holiday, let himself fall headfirst into the channel.

[5]

HARASSED

Sybil, the Professor's wife, had asked her friend Deborah round for morning coffee. Deborah was one of the 'new wives' whom Sybil tried to help settle in when they first arrived. Sometimes it was a bit tricky when their husbands were in Michael's department, but she did her best. This morning, however, it was Sybil herself who was in need of support.

'Of course it's happened before,' she said, 'perhaps more often than I know. It probably doesn't seem very terrible to you, being young – or younger,' she added, for Deborah had two children who were at that moment detained with other offspring at the university crèche.

'Well, I've heard about such things, naturally,' said Deborah, 'though I must say no one ever tried it with me when I was a student. Too much of a plain Jane, I expect.'

'Don't be silly, dear.' Sybil brushed this distraction aside. Deborah was a perfectly nice-looking girl, even if not the kind that tended to catch Michael's professorial eye. 'Before, I knew it would blow over, when I knew at all. But this time it's different. I can tell – you know how one can.'

By now Deborah felt rather out of her depth – her husband was a blameless biochemist who adored his children and for whom family life supplied everything that biochemistry could not – but she murmured sympathetically. 'It must be awful for you. And after all,' she ventured further, 'so undignified for him.'

'Quite – and so bad for the department.' At this point Sybil's pained attempt at composure crumpled; her chin trembled, and her eyes watered. 'It's so hurtful,' she said, 'I feel so hurt. I've never been unfaithful, never wanted to be – haven't much chance now anyway, at my age.'

Deborah didn't know whether to agree with Sybil that she was past the age of attraction, which seemed rather insulting, or to suggest that there might still be possibilities which she was clearly in no mood to welcome.

'It's not that I'm worried that he'll be had up for sexual harassment, or whatever it is they call it now, and it's not that he doesn't love me and all that.' Her eyes watered again. 'It's just that I'm not enough any more, and it makes me think I never was.'

Deborah, who had only known Sybil for a few weeks, could say nothing to this, but she attempted to take her hand instead. Sybil withdrew it after a moment, patted Deborah's wrist perfunctorily in return, and got up from the sofa on which they were sitting.

'I think, in the circumstances, I shall treat myself to a little gin. Would you like some?'

Deborah – anxiously aware that her toddlers would by now be fractiously waiting for the healthy lunch she hadn't yet prepared for them – made her excuses. 'I really must go,' she said, adding in what was intended to be a heartening but compassionate tone, 'would you like me to look in tomorrow?'

'If you like,' said Sybil, 'if you're free, but there's no need. I'll be all right.'

Michael was sitting at his desk in his room at the department, his concentration disturbed after an uneasy lunch with James, his fellow professor. Not that lunches with James were ever very satisfactory, since entirely straightforward questions on some faculty matter were only too likely to precipitate the anguished silences for which he was locally famous. James usually felt that the considerations on both sides of any argument hung in such exquisite balance that he could hardly bring himself to disturb it.

'What's the problem?' said Michael, seeing that James was more than usually put out by something. James winced at the brutality of so direct an enquiry, but he was fond of Michael in spite of everything (as people often were) and even fonder of Sybil, and he made an effort to be forbearing.

'I've wasted the whole morning in this wretched committee.'

'Which committee is that?'

'You know quite well which committee, since I'm only on it because you refused to serve.'

'You mean the committee to draw up guidelines on sexual harassment?'

'Exactly.'

'How are you getting on?'

'If by "you" you mean the committee in general, they seem to be enjoying the task. If you mean me personally, I don't. I find the whole subject distasteful and even distressing.'

Michael knew from James's tone that he expected to be pressed further, and – as they sat over their coffee in the now empty common room – he felt he had to respond. After some ritual skirmishing around the outer works of James's entrenched sense of scruple, what emerged was that he simply couldn't reconcile his own chivalric feeling that there are some things one just can't do with the clear evidence that unethical conduct did sometimes occur. The fact that in some cases it did so in circumstances which were, to say the least, extenuating only made the whole question yet more recalcitrant. Wearily, Michael thought that he'd better bring matters out into the open.

'Look, James, the real problem is me, isn't it?'

James fluttered his hands helplessly.

'I shouldn't dream of descending to personalities.'

'Of course you wouldn't, and I'm grateful. All the same, some of your committee probably think we need this code because of the way I've behaved in the past, and I'm still behaving, for that matter. I know Annette's a postgraduate now, but your colleagues may think she shouldn't be harassed, even so.'

James took off his glasses and began to polish them.

'I'm sorry to embarrass you, but you can hardly not know about her, given our dear secretary's appetite for gossip, and the fact that Annette always phones me here because obviously she can't ring me at home.'

The normal fastidiousness of James's speech-acts was hardly equal to this lurch into candour, and he was reduced to muttering banalities about its not being his business and not wanting to see Sybil hurt.

'Nor do I,' said Michael, 'how could I? But I don't want to hurt Annette either, especially now.'

This was too much for James's curiosity.

'Why now, especially?'

'Because she's pregnant. She told me last week. As you can imagine, it makes things rather difficult.'

James got up from his armchair and began to wander round the room, turning over a periodical or two on the table. Michael watched him but said nothing further. James avoided his eye, but as he made for the door he put his hand on his colleague's shoulder as he passed. 'I wish you'd stick to literature, Michael, and leave life alone,' he said, as he went out.

Michael crossed to the window. It was still fine outside; no sign of the promised rain. He called in at the office to say that he'd be out for an hour or two, but would be back to sign his letters later. If his wife rang, he'd be home at the usual time. Walking away from the department, he felt sure from the studied propriety of his secretary's expression that she knew where he was going. Why couldn't his private life be private?

The house Annette lived in was between fifteen and twenty minutes' walk; it depended which route he took. He always went on foot, never by car – not since he'd been spotted parking by one of Sybil's protégées who'd innocently mentioned the fact to her. It was a pity she'd found out, although she was bound to, sooner or later. Before, he'd been almost relieved when the truth was discovered: it brought him back to Sybil's reliable, if querulous, devotion. This time the shock of the affair and its unexpected consequence had made him feel that he didn't now know where he was or what was going to happen; he was in uncharted territory. His customary confidence that things would work out somehow, that everything would be all right in the end, had deserted him. His usual air of being in control – one of the qualities which made him a lucid and reassuring teacher – was increasingly hard to maintain; he seemed less and less able to exert any will at all. He couldn't leave Sybil. It was so out of the question that it hardly occurred to him even as an option. On the other hand he didn't see how he could abandon Annette. It was perhaps possible that she might go away of her own accord, although it didn't seem likely at the moment. Michael was not self-conscious – that was part of his appeal – but he was not very self-aware either, so that the idea of himself as someone who let others take the crucial decisions was unnerving because it was unfamiliar.

Going up to Annette's room Michael as usual felt furtive, and as usual was annoyed with himself for feeling so. It was a large and much-divided house and one was quite likely to pass someone on the stairs, which could be awkward. But there was no one about, and he paused on the landing outside her door, listening to the sound within.

She was playing the spinet which she'd been given by her father, who made copies of old instruments in his spare time. Michael wasn't musical himself, but he loved hearing Annette play because it made him think of the first time he saw her. He'd gone, out of duty, to a student production of *Measure for Measure*. She didn't have a speaking part and didn't appear until the fourth act when, accompanying herself, she sang 'Take O take those lips away' to an extremely dejected-looking Mariana. 'Very Tennysonian, but where's the moated grange?' said James, who was sitting next to Michael and liked old-fashioned sets. Michael, caught by the way she gazed at Mariana as if she wished to share her desolation, didn't reply. He spent the rest of the performance hoping she'd come on again, and felt extraordinarily rewarded when she finally did so, as an attendant in the last scene. She followed the unfolding of the unlikely dénouement with grave concentration, more like a spectator than an actor. Michael gazed at her continually, aware of the action only as she mirrored it. Going home afterwards, he'd felt inexplicably happy.

The music stopped abruptly, and then began again. Martin opened the door stealthily and leaned back against it on the inside.

'I just can't play today,' she said, without turning her head, 'can't get the ornaments right.'

'I tried to creep in without disturbing you. What's the piece?'

'Don't you recognize it? You're very ignorant, for a professor. It's Couperin – "Le Rossignol en Amour". I specially love this bit, where it says *accens plaintifs*.'

He crossed the room and stood behind her, looking over her head at the music, as she played the bars once more.

'I'm glad it's marked *très tendrement*,' he said, putting his hands on her shoulders. 'What does "Double de Rossignol" mean, on the opposite page?'

'A *double* is a variation. You can play the top line on the flute as well – except that you're so hopeless you can't play a note,' she added, smiling indulgently as she turned round to him, looking up, her eyes full of love. He bent down and kissed her forehead. It was one of those moments when he knew he couldn't do without her.

'I was playing because you hadn't come, and I felt lonely.'

'Well, I'm here now.'

'Would you like some tea, or shall we lie down?'

'Why don't we have some tea, and then lie down?'

As he sat beside her on the bed, one hand holding a cup, the other hand holding her hand, he began tentatively to suggest that they should think about an abortion. It would be terribly upsetting, naturally, but it would surely be best for her, for her career, and – not least – for the unwanted child.

'But it isn't unwanted. I want it,' said Annette gently, but also with a note of firmness which Michael was beginning to realize he had little chance of resisting. 'It's because I want you too,' she went on. She put her hand up to his face and stroked his cheek, as if testing how well he had shaved, before kissing it. There seemed little point in resisting that either, as things now were.

As he lay on his back, he studied the plasterwork on the ceiling, his arm round Annette who lay curled up beside him, her head on his chest. He listened to the noises in the street outside. They seemed to increase, both in volume and distinctness, as the afternoon light retreated. Eventually he made himself look at his watch, although the movement was bound to wake her.

'I really must be getting back,' he said, and only just stopped himself from adding, Sybil will be wondering what's happened to me. That was the trouble with this sort of thing: you had to watch your words all the time.

In fact, Sybil had been wondering about herself rather than her husband – about the self that no longer seemed to have a husband that could be relied on. She began to realize, after the third or fourth gin since Deborah's departure, how much she'd always needed someone on whom she could depend. Why was that? Her early years had been conventionally placid, without any disasters which might have damaged her self-confidence. That had been part of Michael's charm for her: he made her feel that everything was under control, and because of that she'd been able to help others. 'Don't *worry*,' he would say, and she hadn't – not for a long time. Even when she began to admit to herself that his air of calm and competence was really due to the way he ignored anything troubling or inconvenient, she still looked to him to look after her, and she didn't see how he could, now. As she thought about the future, her mind already aswim, she couldn't find a place for herself in it, however hard she tried.

'I suppose I'd better have something to eat,' she said, aloud. Sybil tended to peck at snacks when Michael was out; it didn't seem worth bothering without him. She began, rather guiltily, to make some porridge, as she sometimes did when she felt like

89

being comforted. She liked stirring it and watching the bubbles swell and collapse, as she used to do when she was a child. It tasted a bit odd, after the gin, but when she'd got it down she felt fortified enough to decide what to do next.

She rang James at the department. Fortunately he'd not yet gone home.

'James, I want the address of that girl.'

'What girl?' said James defensively.

'You know, the girl Michael's interested in. Don't be difficult, James, I want to see her and talk to her. Perhaps I can help.'

James tried to work out quickly how much Sybil knew. She sounded rational enough over the phone, and in any case her concern for the welfare of graduates as well as of younger staff was well known. It seemed safe enough, as well as the easiest thing, to give her what she wanted.

Sybil quite enjoyed writing her note. She wanted to sound magnanimous and understanding so that being wonderful about everything would make her still valued by both of them, not realizing that however necessary she was to Michael she was of little interest to Annette. Sybil wasn't sure whether to ask Annette to come round or to suggest that she might call on her; perhaps a meeting on neutral ground would be best. In the end she left the choice to the younger woman.

The feeling that she could hardly be behaving better buoyed her up as she licked the envelope and found a first-class stamp. She didn't lock the front door since the box was almost opposite; there was still time to catch the afternoon post. But, half-way across the road, it suddenly struck her that she really had lost Michael for good this time, that her letter acknowledged the fact, and that therefore she couldn't send it after all. With a sob that was almost a cry she turned round sharply and started to go back, not seeing the lorry until it was too late.

Michael returned to the department to sign his letters and collect his car. When James took him into his room, sat him down, gave him a Scotch, and told him that Sybil had been run over, Michael couldn't at first take him seriously. He kept asking how badly she was hurt, and it was some time before he began to accept even the possibility of her death. Fatal accidents were what happened to other people, that you read about in the papers or saw on the news. And when James went through it all yet again – how the hospital had rung the department and how he personally had spoken to the casualty officer, so that Michael had no choice but to accept a story that James could not conceivably have made up – Michael found he didn't know how to react. Grief, sorrow, and even guilt, would presumably materialize in due course, but for the moment there seemed nothing to feel, and nothing to feel with. It was as if he had come round from an anaesthetic too soon, conscious but nulled.

James was sufficiently alarmed by the blankness of Michael's response to offer to take him back to his own house for the evening so as to keep an eye on him. Normally he never entertained domestically, although whether this was due to the reluctance of his foreign wife – rumoured to be difficult – or simply because he was usually tired and antisocial after a hard day remained unclear.

'It's kind of you, James,' said Michael. 'I'm touched, really – but I'd rather be on my own, what with going to the hospital, and everything.'

He couldn't decide whether to make for home straightaway and face Sybil's absence there, or go and identify what had been Sybil, which he'd have to do sooner or later. At any rate he didn't feel he could drive, so he left the car where it was and began to walk in the opposite direction to that which he'd taken earlier. He struck out across the university park, shuffling through drifts of dead leaves as he used to do when he was a boy. On the other side there was a pub which he often passed but had never been into. It had the kind of Thirtyish windows which Michael particularly hated; inside the overhead lighting was flat, and the general effect municipal. Two or three men sat with their pints in front of them, morosely studying their evening papers.

'What's it to be, squire?' said the barman.

'I think it'll be simpler if I stick to Scotch.'

'Why not? Here you go – one double Scotch. Still fine out, is it? This morning they said we were going to have rain. Never get it right, do they?'

Michael took his drink into a corner, swallowed it as quickly as he could, and then left. Working towards the centre of town, he stopped at three or four other places which proved equally depressing. In one of them, thinking he ought to have something to keep himself going, he ate a bag of crisps. At last he found somewhere with a band which, though small, played so loudly that people could hardly hear themselves speak and mostly didn't try to – a welcome protection against strangers who wanted to chat. It was filling up with young drinkers, but by this time Michael no longer cared whether they might include some of his students. Raising his head, he was surprised to see from a clock on the wall – unnoticed earlier – how much time had passed. Better get to hospital before it's too late. He stumbled over the threshold as he left, bumping into a couple coming in, and caught hold of the man's lapel. He apologized and was about to explain, but then thought better of it.

In the open the air was wonderfully fresh. Perhaps it had rained after all. He bent down and put his hands flat on the pavement to see if it was wet. When he took them away they were quite damp; he pressed them to his face. He felt he could now cope with the formalities at the hospital. When shown Sybil's body he blinked, but otherwise seemed calm. In fact, he was so intent on maintaining his composure that he couldn't concentrate on her expression, or lack of it, as he would have liked.

Michael wasn't far from his house when he suddenly stopped and stood still. Something had come back to him. Instead of the dead Sybil under a sheet that covered all of her except her white face he began to see, with increasing distinctness as the image developed, a living but critically ill Sybil as she had been twenty years ago, after a miscarriage during which she had lost a lot of blood. She was so given up to the pain that she didn't even know he was there. He remembered how passionately he'd wanted to take over the pain, suffer it for her. He had never loved her so much.

He looked along the road. The lights were too faint and too far apart to illuminate it properly. The traffic had thinned out by this time, but he soon saw some headlights coming towards him, quite fast, on his side of the road. A few seconds before the car reached him he stepped off the kerb and into its path. At the last moment, however, it swerved to avoid him and hit a lamp-post, leaving Michael standing. The noise of the crash was extraordinarily loud. In the silence that then flooded back he saw that the street-light – bent but not extinguished by the impact – shone through the broken windscreen of the uptilted car on to the faces of the two passengers inside. They were completely impassive, except that the driver had a severe cut on her forehead from which blood was trickling, soon to congeal.

As he went to look more closely, he had to hold on to the lamp-post while he tried to get his breath back, but it was a long time before he did so.

EARLY RETIREMENT

'Well, what did the doctor say?' asked Hester, helping her husband off with his coat, as she liked to do.

'Just what one would expect, really. Avoid stress, remember that none of us are as young as we used to be, take reasonable exercise – that sort of thing.'

'But did you discuss the early retirement idea?'

'Yes, we did.'

'What did he say?'

'He said that while on the one hand it was worth bearing in mind, on the other hand it might well be premature.'

'That's very helpful.'

'There's no need to be heavily ironic, Hester. It's a matter for me, or rather for us, to decide, not for him. It's quite proper for him to refrain from too positive a recommendation, one way or the other.'

'Your ironies are just as heavy as mine, Philip, and far more frequent. But are you sure that everything is all right?'

'As all right as we can expect them to be, at our age. You mustn't worry, Hester. There's no cause for agitation.'

Still not quite reassured, she put her hands to his face and kissed his forehead. He gently took her hands away but touched one of them with his lips as he did so, as if to offset any suggestion of rejection. They went from the hall into the drawing-room.

'You've lit the fire,' he said. 'How nice. Shall we allow ourselves a drink before supper? I wish the doctor would tell me how to avoid stress on the M4. The traffic coming home was dreadful.'

He continued to sit and sip by the fire when his wife got up to go to the kitchen. He lifted his glass with both hands as if it warmed them, so as to control any suggestion of tremor. So far, so good; it was just a question of keeping it up. He was worried that, in an effort to be normal, he had verged on self-parody just now, his phrasing even more pedantic than usual. Another sign of age, presumably – finding yourself trapped in a syntax you never consciously chose but had got stuck with. Still, Hester seemed to accept his account, for the moment. He didn't like telling her a lie – something that as far as he could remember he had never done – but he didn't feel he had any option. He could hardly explain airily that in fact the doctor had confirmed his own worst fears. He couldn't bear the thought of the pain it would give her, nor of the scene she would have made on hearing the truth.

He had thought about it a good deal in the car on the way back, naturally. He didn't even turn on Radio 3 as he usually did during the early stages of the journey, while the traffic moved spasmodically forward from one set of lights to the next. Whatever happened, there would be some consolation – if of a grim kind – in not having to do this trek so often. When they had moved out into the country on the far side of Henley twenty-five years ago, he had made light of the commuting he'd have to do to the university college where he taught. He could work at home, wouldn't have to go in every day, liked driving anyway, and the motorway would make it seem no farther than the outer suburbs where some of his colleagues lived. But the administrative chores had somehow become more inescapable, and there were many more meetings than there used to be. He thought of going by train so that at least he could read, but it wasn't so convenient, especially now that, through seniority, he had succeeded to one of the college's coveted parking spaces. And the truth was that he liked being alone, in his car, even in the midst of all the other cars. His theory was that it gave him time to think, although in practice he never thought anything really through, under such conditions.

When the traffic was particularly bad he made himself patient by reminding himself that the real reason for moving out of town was to make Hester happy. Brought up in the country herself, she had never taken to London. Philip had never forgotten – often deliberately recalled – the tears in her eyes when, after looking round their house for the first time, he'd said, 'Let's have it, if you really want it.' It was only too like her to show her emotion so transparently, but he was glad that, on that occasion, she'd done so. His joy in her happiness was hardly less than her joy in what seemed like a dream come true, though he showed it less. Knowing that he himself had become more reserved in time, he wondered if she still realized how important her happiness was to him, how it had always been what most mattered. How was he to secure it now?

The doctor hadn't given him six weeks to live, or anything melodramatic like that. It wasn't as if he had developed a cancer which was going to carry him off before he had time to prepare himself. People with *paralysis agitans* could live for a long time; much could be done to control the worst of it; modern drugs were effective and continually improving. At the time Philip had seemed to acquiesce in the doctor's evident wish to make the best of his case, although he privately felt that the tone might have been a little less bracing. No doubt his air of academic detachment made it look as if he was ready to face the future constructively.

His first thought had been, what about Hester? His second was a memory, hidden for years, of an elderly man in the bed opposite him when he himself had been in hospital briefly for a minor operation. The old chap had been suffering from what was now his condition, but in an advanced form. His helplessness, the amount of care he needed, but above all the constant and involuntary shaking of his hands had depressed Philip deeply. He remembered thinking, I hope I never come to that.

There was a hold-up because of a contraflow. While waiting he looked in the driving mirror, adjusting the angle so that he could see his own face. It looked calm enough. He was also aware that it looked what others might call distinguished. He had always been a handsome man, and although this had not been important to him he knew that it had been so for Hester. She had been proud of his looks from the first, embarrassingly so at times. When younger she had often teased him, a classicist by profession, for having so very Roman a nose. Even now, she couldn't resist smoothing his hair – greying but still thick – as she passed, when he was sitting at table or at his desk. He had long permitted these and other caresses indulgently, accepting her need to touch him so often, even though it was not natural for him to show his own love for her in such overt ways.

Accelerating now, he thought again of the old man, and tried to visualize himself reduced to the same state. He held the steering-wheel tighter, so as to test the grip in his fingers. What would it be like, not to be in control any more? Of course, one would approach such a condition gradually so one might adjust by degrees, but he couldn't imagine himself ever becoming reconciled to it. On the rare occasions when he'd been ill hitherto, he had regarded himself simply as temporary host to certain predictable symptoms, tiresome lodgers in his body who would soon decamp, leaving him to get back to being himself. He couldn't take that line any more. What he had now had come to stay.

It wasn't that he was afraid of being dead. Those passages in classical literature which asserted that not to have been born at all was best had always appealed to him. Nor had he flinched from death as an eventuality: his will was in order, and Hester provided for. The superannuation would be adequate, now that the mortgage was nearly paid off, and he'd taken out some extra insurance. He wasn't much older than his wife, but he'd always taken it for granted that he'd die first, dwelling with some satisfaction on the thought that Hester would have no financial anxieties – would indeed be able to afford some luxuries, holidays, good clothes. He didn't like the idea of her comforts being eroded by the nursing-home fees he would have to meet, as his state deteriorated.

Driving over the bridge at Henley, he looked at the river with pleasure, as he almost always did. It was brown and brimming with winter rain, so that the boats moored alongside the street were more on a level with it than usual. One would miss such sights, certainly, if cooped up. It was odd, how long things took to sink in. He began to realize that the early retirement he'd been considering (currently available on attractive terms since official policy was to run down the classics department) was now not just an option but an inevitability. And it wouldn't bring him more freedom, but less. There would come a point when he'd have to stop driving, when it would become increasingly difficult to leave the house, when he'd have to spend more and more time in bed, being nursed, until he finally became too much for Hester to cope with at home. He knew that she would never complain, but how would she really feel, seeing her admired husband weaken and collapse month by month, year by year, into something like the old man in the ward, who might have been good-looking too, and loved, in his day?

The road between Henley and his house had been improved lately and a new lay-by made in which he now stopped for the first time. He had to rest for a moment so as to prepare himself to face Hester with what must be an untroubled air. He turned off the ignition and sat quite still, as if listening intently. It seemed very quiet. Something about his breathing wasn't right; he became aware of his heartbeat, normally never noticed; he tried to swallow and felt a lump in his throat. He realized that he had begun to cry, but was so astonished that at first he made no effort to dry his eyes but let the tears trickle from behind his rimless glasses. He couldn't remember when he had last wept – not since his marriage, anyway. Even his parents' deaths had found him resigned and calm. He had come to think of himself as unshakeably philosophical. What was he crying for? He was crying because he had been told how his life would end, because he had decided he would have to end it, because by ending it he would give his wife terrible pain. All he could do (though she would never know it) would be to lessen that pain by dying sooner rather than later. It was strange how one made decisions: the truth seemed to be that they were made for you, the important ones at any rate, by something within.

He got out of the car and walked along the grass verge, past a large but empty bin marked GRIT, until he came to a gate on which he was glad to lean, the road behind him. The field fell away sharply to a copse at the bottom of the slope which was becoming more obscure as the November day misted up. He closed his eyes and saw Hester far below, in the sharp Greek light and the midday heat, at the amphitheatre at Epidaurus. He had asked her to go down to the orchestra and say something to him, as he looked down from the rear-most circle of seating, to test the famous acoustics. Her figure – so young then, so slight, so beautiful – seemed touchingly diminished by distance, but her words reached him with a startling immediacy. 'Philip, Philip,' she cried as she waved, 'can you hear me? I love you. Can you hear that?' He opened his eyes suddenly and looked back towards the lay-by, worried – now as then – that someone had overheard.

Better get home. Putting it off would only make matters worse. Later that night, as they lay side by side, he surprised his wife by taking her in his arms and holding her with such unusual closeness that she said, with a tenderness that he could only just withstand, 'What is it, Philip? Tell me what's the matter.'

'It's nothing,' he said, 'nothing for you to worry about. You must get some sleep.' But it was he who dropped off first, in the end, as she stroked his forehead with fingers that had never felt more soft.

The progress of his disease did not appear to be particularly rapid, taking one day with another, although the constant concentration needed to detect and disguise his incipient tremor was tiring. There didn't seem any need to do anything before Christmas, a festival to which Philip, with his pagan studies and sympathies, was habitually indifferent, but which Hester was looking forward to because their son, who lived in America, was coming home for a few days. The visit went well, and Philip was almost able to put his situation on one side of his mind, for the moment.

Early in the new year, however, he made himself start thinking about ways and means. Crossing the river so often, he naturally began to wonder whether a drowning accident might not be the best thing – with the Thames as a rather provincial substitute for the Styx – but it wasn't really plausible. He had always been a good swimmer, his strokes cleaving the water cleanly if not with great power, and he did not lack stamina. It was a pity Hester hadn't learnt, despite his efforts to teach her, when younger. She loved the river nevertheless.

'Do you remember that summer when we hired a boat for the whole season?' he said one evening at supper.

'Of course I do. That was just before the baby. You used to row me up river for miles, and then it was easy coming back, with the stream. I wonder what happened to those white trousers you had – you looked so nice in them. You enjoyed it too, didn't you? You didn't just do it for me?'

'No, I liked it. After all I did row at Oxford, though not in a very distinguished boat. I couldn't do it now.'

'Of course you could, darling. Your hands would get sore at first, but they'd soon harden up. Let's try it this summer, when the Regatta's over.'

No, Philip thought, the river was not the answer.

It wasn't long, however, before the elements came to his aid. There was an unusually heavy fall of snow in the Thames Valley in mid-January, and for a couple of days the local roads were almost impassable. From Philip's point of view this didn't greatly matter: he was able to finish off an overdue review of a not uninteresting book on Sophocles, and to work on a lecture he was soon due to give at a German university. By the third day cars were able to move again, if gingerly, and he said to Hester that he ought to try to get in to college.

'I suppose so,' she said, with resigned ruefulness. 'It's been so lovely having you home unexpectedly. It makes me look forward to your retirement even more.'

She put his scarf round his neck and tucked the ends into his coat, studying his face as she always did at parting.

'Did you cut yourself shaving this morning? I wish you'd get an electric razor. I should have given you one for Christmas.'

'You know I don't like them. It's only a nick. My hand must have shaken slightly. Well, I must be off.'

'Do take care, darling. And drive slowly.'

'I will. Don't worry.'

She kissed his forehead as usual; unusually, he kissed her in the same way.

'I love you, Hester,' he said, before he turned to go.

She hardly had time to register her joy at this rare avowal before she heard the car start. Looking through the drawing-room window, she just caught a glimpse of him turning out of the drive. She put on her coat and went out to shut the gate, as she always did when he left.

It must have been about an hour and a half later when the police car drew up. Two officers got out, knocked at the door, and asked if they might come inside. Hester seemed to take the news of the accident quite well, at first. Shortly before the road from the village joined the main Oxford to Henley route there was a steep hill, with a sharp right-hand bend at the bottom. When Philip and Hester first moved to the area they used to refer to it as Dangerous Corner, after the then well-known play. The land dropped further away on the nearside of the road, and the hedge, severely trimmed by machine, had not been substantial enough to prevent the car rolling over several times into the field after skidding on the snow.

'Your husband may have thought the road was gritted, madam,' said the officer, 'but it looks as if they haven't got round to it yet.'

There was a pause, during which Hester stared ahead of her, and said nothing.

'There's just one thing I have to ask, if I may,' the policeman added. 'Was your husband in the habit of fastening his seat-belt? People don't always do it, although it's the law.'

'Oh yes,' said Hester, 'always. He was careful about things like that.'

Hester also held up well during the identification of the body. She wasn't able to say anything, but she nodded when they drew the sheet back. Outside in the corridor, however, she suddenly stopped, as if she had run out of breath, and then crumpled to the floor. It was fortunate that her friend was with her, to take her home.

After this brief collapse Hester was relieved to find that she was able to rise to the occasion of the funeral, helped by her son, who flew over for a couple of days. The number of letters she had to write was surprisingly large. Besides those on financial and legal matters, there were many expressions of sympathy from Philip's colleagues and fellow-scholars, some of whom were hardly known to her, which had to be acknowledged. Hester was so stupefied by her husband's death that all this took time. Her brain worked slowly; she had to rely on pills to get enough sleep. She couldn't bring herself to drink the sherry she used to enjoy sharing with Philip and emptied the half-finished bottle down the sink, but she tried gin instead until she found that the more she had the worse she felt.

It was hard to say which part of each interminable day was the most unbearable. Waking reluctantly out of her drugged stupor to the absence of Philip's body next to hers was probably the worst moment, and one which she couldn't talk about to her women friends, supportive as they were. At first she thought that she would change their double bed for one of the singles in the spare room, but it was too much for her to manage on her own and it was too humiliating to ask someone else to do it for her. She had never liked twin beds anyway, hating it when they had had to accept them when travelling or on holiday. She wept for half an hour one day when she remembered how embarrassed Philip had been, in his English way, when she had made a fuss about not having a *grand lit* in that otherwise very nice hotel in Aix. After a week or two she decided she would show her loyalty to her husband by keeping for the rest of her life to the bed they had shared for so long, even though she had to resort to the girlish expedient of putting a couple of pillows where he had lain, so that she would have something to hold in her otherwise empty arms.

Getting rid of Philip's clothes was an ordeal. She knew it would have been better to have had the lot taken away in one go, but she couldn't face that. As she folded and, where necessary, pressed them, she thought of how he looked when wearing them. She couldn't remember where and when they had bought some of his older things – he never chose clothes on his own – and this was another cause of distress. Still, everything that had to go was cleared out in the end, except for his books; they could find a home in a library later.

The fact that the weather remained wretched didn't help. About a month or so after the funeral Hester was looking out of the kitchen window, slowly drying the plate on which she'd had scrambled eggs for lunch, when some snowflakes began to flurry. It wasn't as heavy a fall as it had been before, but it was enough to focus her mind on the actual accident – something from which she had flinched up to now. What suddenly came back to her was the policeman's question about Philip's seat-belt. It was inconceivable that he should have forgotten to fasten it, in those conditions. He had once come as near to losing his temper with her as he had ever done when she had neglected to do so herself, even though she had only been going down to the village shop. There must have been a reason why he hadn't done it up, and with a cry of, 'Oh no,' she realized what it was. She went upstairs, lay face down on their bed, and wept as she had never yet done, for all her tears.

She went on crying, on and off, for most of the night, and by the morning she had decided she had to do something. She knew now what Philip's parting words to her in the hall that day meant. Because Hester had loved her husband so long and so passionately she felt she could read him almost better than he could himself. Such habits of intuitive understanding didn't suddenly stop because he was dead – especially as he didn't feel dead to Hester but only gone away, not there – so she was sure she was right. What had happened to make him even think of such a thing? She knew he wanted to live, and to live as long as possible, for her. When they had talked about his retiring early, they both knew that the real if unstated motive for doing so was that it would give them more time together, before the final separation. She made another leap in her mind. It was after he had seen the doctor, even if not immediately after. It must have been something he had said.

The doctor could hardly refuse to see his patient's widow, even though she had never consulted him herself.

'I know you must be very busy,' said Hester, 'so I'll come straight to the point. Can you give me some idea of what you said to my husband when you last saw him?'

'What did he tell you himself?'

'He gave me the impression that in your opinion there was nothing much to worry about.' She saw him hesitate. 'I'd like you to tell me the truth. It can't make any difference to him now.'

'Well, I'm afraid his account wasn't correct. I had to explain to him that he was suffering from a degenerative disease for which we have as yet, alas, no cure, though much can be done to alleviate it as it takes its course.'

'You mean he would have got progressively worse. Presumably he would have needed more and more care as he became more and more helpless.'

'Yes, that would have become necessary – as time went on, you know.' The doctor got up from his chair. 'I was very sorry to hear of your husband's accident – it must be a dreadful loss for you – but perhaps it may help you to realize that in some ways it was a merciful release, for both of you.'

Although Hester could see that this attempt at comfort was well meant, it made her so angry that she could hardly get her key in the car door because her hand was shaking so much. But as she made her way back on the motorway along which Philip had so often driven, she had to admit that it was her husband who really enraged her. She started talking to him aloud, as she increasingly did. It wasn't her fault if he wasn't there to answer.

'You're supposed to be an intelligent man, Philip – how could you be so stupid? I know you wanted to spare me, but what for? You didn't think of that.'

She had to brake abruptly to avoid ramming the car in front. Hester had got out of the habit of going up to town, and wasn't used to rush-hour traffic.

'You should have thought it through more carefully, darling,' she went on. 'I wanted to look after you always. What do you think I loved you for, all those years? I'd have cared for you, I'd have nursed you. You think it would have been too much for me, but it wouldn't. I wanted to do it, and because you've stopped me there's nothing else for me to do. I can't get used to it without you – you should have known that. I'll never get used to it, never.'

Hester's eyes filled with tears which blurred her vision of the road, so that she had to pull over to the nearside lane. She left the motorway, driving more and more slowly, and reached Henley. She parked near the bridge, and walked by the side of the river for a few yards. The water was still high, and the depth of its colour made it look impenetrable. The light was beginning to go. Another middle-aged woman, out with her dog, came and stood beside her.

'Doesn't look very inviting, does it?' she said. 'Not at this time of year, not like the summer. Do you come here in the summer?' she added, since Hester did not at first reply.

'Sometimes,' said Hester, clearing her throat, 'now and then.'

'Time to get back and make the tea,' said the other woman. The dog perked up its ears. 'Ready for your lord and master.' The dog wagged its tail. 'Besides, it's getting chilly. I shouldn't stay out here for long if I were you.'

Hester drove through the dusk with extreme care until she got to the top of the hill. She felt the road begin to slip away beneath the car with relief. As her speed increased, so did her sense of exhilaration. The darkening hedges peeled off either side of her, split by the car's headlights. She couldn't see beyond their limited beam, and didn't want to. She opened her window to listen to the air as it rushed past. As the dangerous corner approached she took her foot away from the brake, let go of the steering-wheel, and put her hands up to her face.

[6]

NIGHT THOUGHTS

They often went to bed on the early side so as to have time to read. It was one of the things about their life that she most enjoyed. When they were first married she felt shy about wearing her glasses in bed, thinking them unromantic, until one day he happened to say how touching he thought she looked with them on, although he couldn't explain why. She liked him to remove them gently – with both hands, as opticians do – before they turned to other things. It became a little ritual for them.

Sometimes they wouldn't speak for a long while, absorbed in their different books, but she didn't mind that because they were otherwise so close. She loved the stillness of their bedroom at the back of the house which the muffled noise of cars in their quiet street only seemed to deepen. He preferred to sit upright, against the headboard; she half-lay lower down, propped on three or four pillows, so that it was easy for her to lean her head on his chest, and for him to put his right arm round her. They would remain like this for a few moments after putting their books aside, and as they did so the muscles in her neck and shoulders lost their accumulated tension in the drowsiness that began to overtake her.

Jonathan had sent her his new volume of poems as she knew he would, and her husband was reading them. It was his first for five or six years but some of it had been written even earlier, either when they were still together, or soon afterwards. Turning over the pages herself she recognized several poems she'd seen in manuscript, but she didn't tell her husband this. She didn't really want him to read them at all and probably he didn't either, but with his usual magnanimity he would be sure to find something generous to say. Finally she put down her own book because she couldn't concentrate on it any more, and said, 'Well, what do you think?'

'They're impressive, aren't they?'

'I'm not sure. Don't you think the poems are too much the same? And they seem very self-pitying, as usual.'

'Well, perhaps, but surely that's partly the result of the intensity.'

'Yes, he has that – he always had that.'

'It can't be easy for you to judge, darling. Anyway, let's hope he gets some good reviews. It was nice of Jonathan to send it.'

He smiled down at her, in his benevolent way; she looked back at him almost apologetically, but comforted. She was so grateful not to have to say anything further, not to have to argue about it, not to be questioned.

They settled beneath the bedclothes. His breathing soon slowed to its familiar nocturnal rhythm, but she continued to lie awake. Every time sleep felt nearer she tried to run towards it, but it eluded her. Of course the book had disturbed her, as he must have known it would; that was why he'd sent it. It was typical of him not to let things be. Or maybe it was just that they could never let each other be. Even now she didn't understand what it was they had wanted from each other, although at the time she would have done anything for him, and he did everything for her that he could do.

It was obvious that the poems written to her, or about her, were the best. The titles gave nothing away, but she knew which they were. They'd been so happy in those days, before it all went wrong, that she couldn't imagine anything beyond it. She was happy in her present marriage too, never happier, but it was different. She couldn't lead a double life even in her mind – she wasn't like that – but all the same it depressed her to think that you can't have two such happinesses at once, that one must displace the other, so that you were bound to lose. Her friends said that Jonathan had become impossible, and that she was right not to go on. He seemed to be content now, with his new wife, as she was, with her husband. It was silly to worry about it. But as she lay there in a dark faintly illumined by the changing digits on the clock radio, she was troubled because she'd always wanted to love so as to make her life whole, and it hadn't happened. She would have liked her love and her identity to have become one and the same, but part of her self was Jonathan's and would remain so. There was the proof, printed on the page. There was nothing she could do about it, but she wished she could start again and give all she was to the man she now loved lying beside her, sinking deeper into his rest.

He lay on his back, his arms by his side, as he usually did. She put her left hand on top of his right, but gently, so as not to disturb him. She longed for him to wake nevertheless, because she felt lonely and was beginning to panic about not sleeping. It was already too late to take a pill: she had things to do in the morning and had to be alert.

Reading the poems might not have been so bad, for all their one-sidedness, if she hadn't also seen Jonathan that evening on television. It was before her husband had got home – he'd been kept late, as he increasingly was. She wanted to catch the news, but had got the wrong channel. Jonathan was being interviewed by a psychiatrist who clearly assumed that getting at the life would explain the work, although it was equally plain that he was more curious about the one than the other. Always reticent in public at least, Jonathan parried his probes warily.

'Many would say that the most striking part of your new book is the sequence of poems under the title *Absence*. Are they particularly important to you?'

'All the poems in the book are important to me.'

'I ask because you have, I think, been married twice, and it would seem natural to conclude that the sequence had some connection with that.'

'Absence of one kind or another is something most people have to get used to, sooner or later. Besides . . .'

Jonathan had been picking his words with studied care, but now dried up completely. He gazed round the studio in apparent abstraction before staring straight at the lens of the camera. He blinked once or twice, and then refocused. The way the light in his eyes changed for a second or two made her certain that he was really looking at her, as if he still loved her, as if she had that instant come into the room where he was writing, through the open frame that her screen had momentarily become.

Jonathan turned back to the interviewer.

'I'm sorry, I can't answer your question. Actually, I dislike confessional verse. I think the writer's job is to dramatize. Each of my poems has its own speaker, who shouldn't be confused with the private person behind him who finds words for him to say.'

She switched off the set abruptly, having heard that sort of thing often enough before. Jonathan always argued that the artist should be impersonal, but in practice no one was less detached then he was.

In the bathroom she let the cold water run through her hands, and the sensation reminded her of sitting by a stream in the mountains, years ago. They'd been to see the ruins of a nunnery. She'd envied the sisters the single-mindedness of their devotion; Jonathan said that the peace of their life meant a retreat from what most mattered in it. And yet in those days it was their own happiness that had sometimes seemed transcendental.

She pressed her face with a damp flannel, and pushed her hair back from her forehead. Standing by the full-length first-floor window in the drawing-room, she watched for the arrival of her husband's car in the street below. It was beginning to get dark, but she didn't put on the light. There was something about the room's proportions and volume which had calmed her at first sight, nor did she ever tire of its detail; she had it redecorated almost every year. When she'd looked up at her husband and he, seeing how her eyes shone, had said, 'We can't really afford it, but we've got to have it,' her love for him was almost like worship. And they'd been so happy since, in this house, happier than anyone she knew. But she wished, more and more, that it could always have been like that, from the beginning, without her having to go through her other life first. It was such a pity.

She wiped her eyes on the top of the sheet and tried to press closer to him, but wasn't able to do so without making him stir.

'What is it, darling? Are you all right?'

'It's nothing. I just couldn't get off, that's all.'

'Poor darling, I'm so sorry.'

He turned towards her, still hardly awake.

'I love you so much,' she said, 'so much, so much.'

'I know you do. I love you too. Don't get upset. Try to sleep now.'

He put his arms round her, and they began to drift away together. She felt safe.

LIEBESTOD

The pain had become so bad in the last few days that she was not surprised. By the time she had got him sitting up in bed he looked exhausted. Propped against the pillows, his eyes closed, he slowly got his breath back. She sat on the edge of their bed and waited, holding his hand. When he opened his eyes he looked at her and said, 'I can't go on like this any more – really I can't. I think the last day is at hand.' He lifted his eyebrows for a moment, as he always did when quoting or being ironic.

'Perhaps you'll feel a bit better after breakfast. What would you like?'

'I'll tell you what I'd like,' he said, as if requesting something distinctly out of the way. 'I wouldn't mind some porridge. Have we got any?'

She didn't remind him that he'd asked for some only last week. She'd got it in specially. When she came back with the bowl he hadn't moved at all, and she wondered if he'd fallen asleep again.

'No, I'm still here,' he said, opening his eyes. 'It's not quite so bad if I don't move. What about you,' he added, when he'd eaten as much as he was going to, 'have you had some? It's very soothing. I used to love it as a child, especially when I was unhappy, which was most of the time.'

'I had something earlier, before you woke.'

A little later he said, 'It's not the day for the doctor, is it?'

'No, he comes tomorrow.'

'Good. He's a nice man, but I don't want to see him any more. He hates him who would upon the rack of this tough world stretch him out longer – isn't that what Kent says? When did we last see *Lear* anyway?'

'It was at the Old Vic – don't you remember? You seemed very moved at the time.'

'Well, now I know how he felt, even though I haven't got any pelican daughters myself. The trouble with suffering is that it makes you vain – only the best comparisons will do.'

She stroked his hair, still thick, though white.

'You always were vain, darling.'

'Yes, that's true. It's being a poet that does it. Look at me – how alive I am, how sensitive – so much more so than you, dear reader – and I've got all these poems to prove it! Ridiculous, really.'

He closed his eyes again for a time, and then rallied.

'I should have written less, more carefully.'

'Some of your work is good – you know that.'

'Well, perhaps, but will it go on being good?'

'I don't know – no one can – but I hope the best of it will last.'

'Leave it to time, that old common arbitrator. As if there was anything else to leave it to.'

She changed the subject. 'Do you think you'll feel like getting up, later on?'

'Of course. Must get up, today of all days. But I'll stay here until after lunch.'

She left the bedroom door open lest he should call, while she tidied up round the flat. She would hear him two rooms away, although his voice was weak and papery now. It wasn't just that the old power had gone, but he'd also lost his actorish habit of moving rapidly from one register to another. Although he'd been a successful public reader of his own verse, he'd always been a bit embarrassed by his histrionic tendencies even as he gave way to

118

them. 'Pure ham, I'm afraid,' he would murmur to his neighbour on the platform, while the audience clapped. She wondered if his recordings of his better-known pieces would help his reputation in the long run.

The morning passed quickly enough. She rang the surgery to make sure that the doctor would call the next day, cancelled the milk and the newspaper, and wrote various notes. The most important letters – to those closest to them – had already been written, so all she had to do was to add the date. She'd prepared them in advance so that she could be at his side as much as possible when the time came.

By midday all the rooms were in order, even his study, with its crowded shelves. He'd hardly picked up a book since the spring, although she read to him a good deal. She'd never cared much about the flat anyway, not as she had about the cottage. Leaving the country had been hard, but it was too isolated where they were, too far away from the treatment he needed.

After washing up the lunch things she began to get him out of bed. Some days he was so irritable she dreaded washing and dressing him. She felt that he used the pain as an excuse for being inconsiderate, even though she knew how intense it was, and would have done anything to make it less. But today he was patient and courteous, more like his old self.

'Shall I put a tie on, for a change – what do you think? If it's not too much trouble. You choose.'

'What about this one? We got it in that craft shop in Pembrokeshire – you know, the place with all those hideous toasting-forks with pixies on them.'

'Impossible to forget – they struck terror to the soul. They would have made Faustus himself think twice.'

'There. Is that comfortable – not too tight?'

'No, that's fine. How do I look?'

He smiled at her with ironic self-admiration. His eyes were bluer than she had ever seen them. She felt flooded with happiness.

'It's all right, darling,' he said, reaching out for her hand. 'It'll be all right.'

119

'I know,' she said, as she kissed his forehead. 'Now, should you like to sit by the window? It seems quite bright outside.'

Their living-room had a pair of french windows which opened on to what from below looked like a balcony, although it was little more than a balustrade. Since he'd been confined to the flat he'd taken to stationing himself there, on fine days. 'How fearful and dizzy it is to cast one's eyes so low,' he would say, 'even though we're only on the first floor.' He liked to watch the comings and goings in the street beneath and dramatized them unscrupulously. 'Look,' he said, 'there's the woman from number seventeen again, going to see her friend in number twenty-nine. I wonder why he never visits her. Anyway, she'll come out just before the kids come home from school, looking flustered. That's the trouble with making love in the afternoon – there's still the rest of the day to get through.'

She couldn't stop herself saying, 'That may have been your problem, but not mine.'

He was immediately contrite. 'Forgive me, darling. The older I get the more thoughtless I become. I just got carried away, as usual. Don't leave me.'

She put her hand on his shoulder.

'In fact, we'll all get carried away, sooner or later. Sooner, in my case,' he added.

'And in mine.'

He put up his hand to take hers.

'You don't have to, you know. You can always change your mind. Why not hang on, and I'll just forge ahead, on my own?'

'There's no point in going on without you.'

She still stood behind him, looking out over him as he sat. He kissed her hand several times, and pressed it to his cheek.

'I love a soft September day,' he said. 'Best time of the year, really. I know it gets dark earlier, but who wants a long twilight? It isn't the winter evenings that make the Scandinavians suicidal, it's the midnight sun.'

The traffic in the street began to increase as its residents returned from shopping or work, to stay in and watch television,

120

or to change and go out again, to dinner, to the theatre, to meet friends.

'It's all very well of Coleridge to talk about the numberless goings-on of life, but there can't have been much happening at midnight in Nether Stowey, especially if it was frosty. Here, there would be some truth in it.'

'Don't talk too much yourself, darling. You'll get tired.'

'I've tired the sun with talking and sent him down the sky.'

He raised his eyebrows, but she shook her head, not catching the allusion.

'Don't you know it? "They told me, Heraclitus, they told me you were dead" and so on – it's in Palgrave's *Golden Treasury*. You're too young to have been brought up on it as I was. Too marmoreal, really – or perhaps one should say lapidary. Tiresomely memorable, though.'

He closed his eyes suddenly and grimaced, until the spasm eased.

'I think I've had enough air. Let's close the windows. These pain-killers he's given me are just hopeless, no good at all.'

'Do you want to lie down for a bit?'

'No, no, I'd prefer to stay in here.'

He managed to stand up at the third attempt with her help, and then, using his walking frame, crossed the room to the sofa.

'How I hate this thing. Put it where I can't see it, will you?'

The sofa had a high back so that he could rest his head against it while watching, or half-watching, the television set in front of it, his feet warmed by the electric fire alongside. She finally got him settled, and then went off to get their customary tea and toast. When she came back, his breathing seemed quicker and more shallow.

'Shall I pour your cup?'

'It's so kind of you, darling, but could you leave it for a moment? Come and sit beside me.'

She held his hand once more, as she waited.

'I think now would be a good time, if you're ready.'

'I am ready.'

121

'And you're sure?'

'Yes, I'm sure.'

'Are you sure you're sure?'

They looked at each other with joy, their faces transfigured, because of the memory his phrase brought back.

She left the room for a minute or two. 'I'm glad you're back,' he said, when she returned. She smoothed his hair away from his brow. 'I'm always here,' she said.

'It's been a lovely day. Thank you.'

He turned his head towards her as she sat down beside him, his eyes looking into hers.

'If you open your mouth I'll put the pill under your tongue, and then I'll do the same.'

'I understand. You know I love you.'

'I know. I love you too.'

When they were found the next day – sitting together still, her arm round his neck, his head on her shoulder – they looked almost as they might have done on any evening in the last year or two, except that the screen was blank and the fire switched off.

[7]

Still ist die Nacht, es ruhen die Gassen,
In diesem Hause wohnte mein Schatz;
Sie hat schon längst die Stadt verlassen,
Doch stect noch das Haus auf demselben Platz.

Da steht auch ein Mensch und starrt in die Höhe,
Und ringt die Hände vor Schmerzensgewalt;
Mir graust es, wenn ich sein Antlitz sehe –
Der Mond zeigt mir meine eigne Gestalt.

Du Doppelgänger, du bleicher Geselle!
Was äffst du nach mein Liebesleid,
Das mich gequält auf dieser Stelle
So manche Nacht, in alter Zeit?

Heine, 'Der Doppelgänger'

The night is still, the streets are at rest,
my sweetheart lived in this house.
Long ago she has left the town,
but the house still stands where it always stood.

And there stands a man, who gazes upwards
and wrings his hands with grief and pain;
I shudder when I see his face:
the moon shows me my own features and form.

You ghostly double, pale companion –
why do you ape the pain of love
that tortured me, in this very place,
so many nights in times gone by?

Translated by S. S. Prawer

AN DIE FERNE GELIEBTE

I waited so long, hoping you'd phone, that I nearly missed the boat. Didn't you get my message? I tried everywhere I could think of. I warned you in my letter that I'd be off to France soon; you might have replied. I wish you'd rung. I stayed in all afternoon, just in case, while I began to pack (I know I've left behind lots of things I'll need). In the end I sat down by the phone and kept muttering please ring now, we must talk before I go, can't you hear me, and so on, as if I could at least reach you by telepathy. I felt ridiculous of course, but there you are. Do you remember how you rang me on impulse once, and couldn't get through because I was trying to phone you at the same moment? I wish you'd got in touch. I'm sure you would have done if you'd realized how I felt, how hurt I was that you didn't.

*

The journey down here was awful, and not only because you weren't with me, as we'd originally planned. I'm still shaken up by it. The crossing was rough, for a start – September equinoctial gales, said someone in the bar, as we steadied ourselves against the roll of the ship with a Scotch or two. I wasn't actually sea-sick, but I certainly felt strange. Even the crew looked a bit subdued. As I walked up

127

the tilting deck past the bookstall a stand of paperbacks on casters almost crashed into me. The girl apologized and put it where she could keep an eye on it; it likes to go walkies when it's choppy, she said. The idea of innocent passengers being assaulted by runaway best-sellers rather appealed to me. Wasn't there some French composer who was killed when a bookcase fell on him? Alkan, I think. Literature is obviously more dangerous than one might think.

The second thing was this terrible hotel. To be fair, the hotel itself wasn't so bad, but it was Saturday night and the place was taken over by a wedding party. I seemed to be the only person present who hadn't known the happy couple intimately since childhood. Dinner was interminable, but the real trouble was the dance afterwards. I'd forgotten how rowdy the French can be on such occasions. It was at least three in the morning before the guests stopped tramping up and down the corridor outside my room. I suppose it was a useful reminder that French provincial life isn't all peace and quiet. If you'd been with me you'd have probably joined in and had a great time. Perhaps it's the effect of spending so much of my life in libraries, but I get upset by too much noise and too many people these days. Premature middle age, you'll say, typical of academics. I think it's just because I'm so on edge all the time.

Anyway, I wasn't feeling too good on the following day when the next disaster struck. I was pottering gently along one of those endlessly straight roads south of the Loire when I was overtaken by some *salaud* in a huge Citroën driving much too fast for a road that had just been resurfaced. A handful of *gravillons* flew up and shattered the windscreen of my already battered Mini. It's very unnerving: one minute you see clearly, the next your vision literally goes to pieces, the image fractured all over by the crazing of the glass. I had to wait an extra day in the first town I came to because they hadn't got a replacement in stock. The man in the garage obviously thought that anyone eccentric enough to drive an English car must expect problems. No doubt the insurance will cover it, but it's a nuisance, now that I've arrived and want to settle in – not easy in any case.

*

The only hotel in St Pierre-des-champs is the one you'll remember from last year, but I didn't feel I could stay there, not on my own, so I've taken a room above the café-bar in the main square, for the moment. It's scruffy, but I like it because I can sit at my window and watch the comings and goings in the *place* below. They park their cars in the middle, and then disappear under the arcades on their errands or assignations. I wait for their return, but I think about you. However, it's too noisy for me to work there, and I'll have to find somewhere else soon.

I start in earnest next week. I've already been out to the Maison Laroche to make arrangements with Madame Lambert, who looks after the family home and guards the Laroche papers. She was scrupulously polite, and I put on my best behaviour in return. I'll be allowed to work in the library every weekday morning and in the afternoons when convenient. She clearly wants to be told what I discover, if anything; I get the feeling I'm strictly on probation. I explained that initially I'll be sorting out Laroche's manuscripts, letters, notebooks, and so on, and trying to put them in chronological order. When I've got some idea of what's there, I'll begin transcribing the more important items. I don't think she actually knows very much about her poet-ancestor or about the Romantic period in general, but she seems very possessive all the same. This may account for the fact that all this stuff has hardly been looked at before. She probably realizes that I'm not academically well established enough to force her hand over possible publication if anything interesting does turn up – and as a foreigner I'm at a dis-advantage anyway. A lot of the work will be boring and mechanical, but I shan't mind that, for the time being. I need anodyne tasks.

*

Today was a good day, as my days go, to start with. I was almost happy. Madame Lambert doesn't like me to arrive too early, and by the time I was on the road to the Maison the mists in the hollows had rolled away; when I got out of the car the late September sun felt really warm. In the woods I pass through, between the two St

129

Pierres, the fading leaves looked so beautiful against the sky, those that were still hanging on in spite of the light breeze. I wondered if the weather in England was as good, knowing how you love a fine morning.

When I got to the library the sun was still low enough to shine well into the room, and I sat on the window-seat rather than at the desk. The view of St Pierre-la-forêt can't have changed much since Laroche's day. He must often have sat here in the house he built, as I do, with a letter in his hand in my hand. I feel increasingly close to him; he's my companion.

It's very quiet in the library, apart from the usual outdoor hum of the south when I have the window open, and the odd snatch of Madame Lambert's voice as she chats to the cleaning woman. The cat, who has taken to visiting me most mornings, dozes beside me on the seat-cushion. The sense of the place and the moment is so strong it's like a weight on me long longed for, almost as if you were lying half across me, your head on my chest – but I mustn't think about that. Is the cat real, at least? I stroke it and it begins to purr but doesn't open its eyes. I shut mine, and wonder if Jean-Philippe, sitting here, had thoughts like mine.

When I stood up to put the papers back in the desk drawer I felt quite dizzy for a few seconds. I went unsteadily across the room to the huge open fireplace, and leant my head against the great beam that spans it. There's always a faint smell of wood-smoke in the room, and on the iron plate let into the stone hearth there was a small mound of ash. The black fire-back had some figures in bas-relief on it, but I couldn't make out what they were. I must ask Madame Lambert about them. Perhaps they date from Laroche's time, or even earlier.

*

I realize I'll have to eke my memories out, if they are to see me through. I try to dwell on only one each day. I take it out of my album with extreme care, turning it round and holding it up to the light, in case I've missed something.

Today I've been thinking about how, when we were staying in

Cornwall, we were woken in the small hours by the brightness of the moon, shining through a gap in the curtains. You turned to me and felt my face. 'Is this really you?' you said. I touched your breast. You sat up, alert. 'Listen,' you said, 'it's the sea – can't you hear it?'

Perhaps it's not a good idea to be as happy as I was then, since it hurts so much later, when you know it hasn't lasted, that it couldn't last, that nothing like that can last.

But although I try to restrict myself to one moment at a time, it always brings back others. When I found you warm beside me after our first night together I thought I'd never be lonely again. I said so when you woke up. You didn't reply but put your fingers across my mouth instead. At the time I thought they were just for me to kiss; now I understand what you meant. It's better not to say such things, not out loud.

*

As you'll see from the address, I've found somewhere to live – and just as well, since evenings at the café have been getting me down, now that it's getting dark earlier and I can't look out on to the square in the evenings.

I rent two rooms in the house of Monsieur and Madame Charpentier. It's on the outskirts of St Pierre, far enough up the hill to see across the town's roofs to the bridge over the river on the far side. The house itself is tall and ungainly – turn of the century probably – but the ceilings are high, even on the top floor where I live, and it's warm. This is because (despite his name) Monsieur Charpentier is a superior sort of plumber specializing in central heating, and he obviously believes that *chauffage* begins at home. In fact I hardly ever see him: he's long gone by the time I surface in the morning, and in the evening he retires to a sanctum at the back of the house into which – given the impenetrability of French private life – I haven't been and don't expect to be invited. I do sometimes pass him in the yard alongside where he stores his materials – piping, radiators, baths, tiles, and so on. He touches his cap and murmurs, 'M'sieur,' amiably enough, but that's all. Madame Charpentier, on the other hand, seems to like having a lodger to chat to. She misses her son and daughter who have both married and gone to live in the city. When they're due to visit on a Sunday, Madame prepares enough food for a siege, and I live off the remains for several days.

So it's cosy, and I'm looked after, but as I work I wish I could stretch out and take your hand under the table as I used to, in the library, when I first knew you.

*

When I moved in I thought I'd enjoy making my own coffee in the morning, but Madame Charpentier offered to bring me a cup instead and I accepted – otherwise some days I'd never get up and on with what I'm supposed to do. As I lie there, waiting for her knock, I think about you and wonder if you think about me. We've been too close for you not to do so sometimes, but you're better at keeping things out of your head than I am. If I was as much in your mind as you are in mine you'd be here, with me, as we agreed.

I wonder too how you'll receive this letter, and all my letters. I suppose it's something one never does know. Perhaps you just glance at them, or even – seeing my handwriting and the French stamp – leave opening them and put them on one side, to be read later, if at all. But I hope you do read them, and even re-read them, so that perhaps you'll come to understand what they really say. If you did, you'd reply, and I shouldn't feel, as I do now, that every time I take a fresh page I'm looking into an abyss.

*

When I arrive at the Maison Madame Lambert greets me with her invariable courtesy, we exchange pleasantries about the weather, she shows me into the library, and then she usually leaves me undisturbed for the rest of the morning. Today she came back an hour later for some reason but, as soon as she opened the door and saw me at Jean-Philippe's desk, she became too flustered to say what it was. I asked her if anything was the matter. 'J'avais cru un instant

132

que c'était lui,' she explained. 'Venez. Je vais vous montrer quelque chose d'étonnant.' She took me into a small sitting-room, full of her own things, which I hadn't been in before. 'Voilà!' She pointed to a framed sketch hanging on the wall, clearly drawn from life. It was a picture of Laroche himself, dashed off in pen and ink by a friend, sitting at the same desk as I was using, writing, as I had been. Didn't I find the resemblance remarkable? I went up to the picture and examined it; I said I couldn't see it myself. Ah, she exclaimed, it's just the same with my brothers – they can't see the likeness everyone else notices. But as I continued to demur she began to waver, conceding that perhaps it was only the attitudes that were similar.

Nevertheless, when I went back to the library I felt unnerved. It was as if my appeals to you were no more than futile echoes of Jean-Philippe's cries to his own distant beloved, made so long ago and (as far as I could discover) with equally little effect. He seemed altogether too close for comfort, this time. I broke off for lunch earlier than usual.

*

The next day I had a bit of a shock myself. I stopped on the way home to get a bottle of wine – well, several bottles; I seem to get through them rather quickly. The supermarket reminds me of the one we used to go to, late in the afternoon, after our swim, after we'd dried on the grass in the sun. It's got the same profusion of vegetables, the same absurd number of cheeses, and the same ceaseless muzak, interrupted only by honeyed invitations to *madame* to *profiter* from the week's special offers. I loved watching you move along the stacks, stretching out your arm, so brown, knowing exactly where, under your T-shirt, the brown stopped. I'm sorry – I know I shouldn't think of such things now, but they're hard to suppress. Anyway, I had just reached for some bottled *haricots* (handy for my solitary suppers) and was looking round for some tinned *pâté* when I suddenly caught sight of you. I blinked, but I was sure it was you. You had your back to me, and seemed to be discussing something with the white-coated butcher behind the meat counter – the thickness of the *escalopes* he was cutting perhaps. I began to move towards you, about to say your name, when you turned to go and it wasn't you. The T-shirt was like the one you used to wear, and her height and hair were similar. I pretended to read the instructions on a packet of pasta and hung on to the shelf with both hands until you'd threaded the checkout. I suppose I may have had too much to drink at lunch. Outside, I had to sit in the car for quite some time before I drove slowly off.

It would be so much easier if you'd write – just a few lines, anything. It's not much to ask.

*

Jean-Philippe's poems are usually dismissed as sentimental but I find them more and more affecting, despite their lachrymose and self-pitying titles – 'Adieu', 'Absence', 'Soupir', 'Le Crépuscule', and so on. I keep hoping I'll find some evidence about what lies behind them, if anything. Was he simply imitating the German poets he admired (like Müller, Rellstab, and most of all Heine), or did he write like that because he really was in love in some hopeless way? I'd like to believe the latter – for obvious reasons – but I can't say I've found any clues so far. Laroche stopped writing this sort of poem some time before his satisfactory but not apparently exciting marriage, and didn't do so afterwards. An earlier attachment seems quite likely, despite the lack of proof. After all, there are lots of reasons why love-letters don't survive, especially if the person they're written to didn't marry the writer in the end, or never cared for him much in the first place.

Admittedly the diction is derivative, but that doesn't mean that the emotion wasn't authentic. The poems may be no more than exercises in a currently fashionable style – expressions of what Laroche felt he ought to feel, but didn't really. On the other hand they could reflect a genuine anguish which he wasn't a good enough poet to convey with the originality which is so often confused with sincerity. Nothing is more humiliating about love than the banalities it drives you to, as I'm afraid you know only too well. When I write to you the words always let me down as they never used to when we were so close we didn't need them anyway.

*

I've had a visit from Mike, of all people – not the first person you'd expect to meet in the depths of provincial France, as you can imagine. He and Celia stopped overnight on their way to a fortnight's sun and sand. They're still together, more or less.

We had a lengthy dinner at the hotel after I'd spent the afternoon showing them the local sights, such as they are. I don't think Mike took much in, and Celia mostly wandered off on her own, but they said they enjoyed the meal. It was a great relief to me to have friends to talk to in my own language for a change. We were well into the second bottle when Celia got up abruptly from the table, saying that she was tired and was going to bed. 'Of course, darling, off you go,' said Mike, as if this was nothing unusual. As she disappeared I poured ourselves another glass.

'Celia looks marvellous, as always.'

'Yes, she's fine. Her career's going rather well at the moment. That's why we couldn't get away earlier – she's been recording something for television. It's a real break for her.'

He didn't sound as pleased about this as I should have expected, and there was a pause while he looked round the now almost empty dining-room.

'What's the problem?' I've had long experience of Mike's problems, and recognized the signs.

'I don't know – something's not right. Celia and I get on very well and all that, but I can't get used to her life somehow. People think it must be exciting to live with an actress – and it is, in a way – but it's very unsettling. When I ring her at the theatre or the studio, she sounds so distant it's as if she's in another country. Sometimes – particularly when she's rehearsing – I don't feel sure of who she is any more.'

'That's natural enough: she's trying to work out how to become someone else.'

'I know, but where does that leave me? It's a bit rough, living with someone who's not really there.'

'Not so bad as not living with someone who you want to be there but isn't.'

'Well, that's true I suppose. We'd better finish this bottle off. Anyway, how's your research going?'

So I told him about all that, glad to get away from such a dangerous area. Fortunately Mike is too self-absorbed to probe much into the lives of others.

I saw them off the next day. The morning was bright and fresh. They seemed happy and excited about their trip. Celia had slept well, and looked even more wonderful. As they sat in their car peering at the map, she leaned her head on his shoulder, and he absent-mindedly kissed her hair. I turned away, although of course I was glad for them. They should have reached the Mediterranean by now.

I hadn't thought of it before, but there's nothing to stop me taking a few days off and going to the sea myself – it isn't that far – but what would be the point, on my own, especially after last time?

*

It's hard for me to imagine what your life is like now because you don't write and so I've nothing to go on, but I try not to in any case because I don't know if you're still on your own. I feel there's bound to be someone else since I can't think of you as unloved, although I doubt if anyone could love you as I did. It's something I've got to face sooner or later, I suppose – the idea of that other, in my place. No wonder I live so much in our past.

*

Last night Madame Lambert invited me to dinner. It was strange going back to the Maison in the evening. The house looked even more isolated than usual in the twilight, the evergreens round it (planted by Laroche himself it seems) giving it a sombre air not apparent during the day. As I got out of the car someone – a woman,

136

I think – who had been watching me arrive from an upper window withdrew, pulling in the shutters after her; I didn't know who she was. The other guests were Madame's sort of age and clearly old friends. As the only younger person there I felt a bit *de trop*, almost as if I were being vetted, although everyone was extremely polite. The meal itself was unpretentious, but better cooked than any I've had here. As Madame served it all herself it took a long time.

We adjourned at last to the *salon* which is dominated by Laroche's grand piano, a highly decorated Erard almost as old as the house – not very well in tune, but with the wistful timbre of the period. Madame Lambert was pressed to sing and, after some token reluctance, agreed to; this was evidently an established ritual. Sometimes, in the library, I'd heard her practising in the distance and one day when she seemed in a more approachable mood I asked her whether she had trained as a singer. Yes, she said, but that was when she was young, in what she called her other life. She didn't elaborate. She must have had a lovely voice then, and although it's frail and insecure now, it still has a silvery purity about it.

She began with Schubert, went on to some Fauré (whose accompaniments rather defeated her elderly pianist), and ended with Beethoven's *An die Ferne Geliebte*, sung in French. She took the opening section so slowly that I wondered if she'd ever get through it, but she made you feel the longing in the music nevertheless. During the Andante she gazed upward at the room's elaborate cornice, her eyes shining. After battling bravely through the final Allegro molto she left us abruptly, sniffing a little, holding her lace handkerchief up to her face. We clapped gently to cover her exit, which seemed to be expected. I asked her friend, sitting next to me, if Madame was all right. Don't worry, she said, it was always the same with that piece: 'Elle pense à son mari.' Had she been widowed long? 'Mais oui, il est mort depuis dix ans.'

I was about to enquire further when our hostess returned with fresh coffee and a plate of *petits fours*. Later I went over to the piano and looked at the music left on the top. The French translation of the Beethoven had been written in under the German words in a hand I recognized immediately. In an early edition of Schubert's

Schwanengesang Laroche had also written in his own versions of two of the Heine poems – 'Ihr Bild' (in which the lover dreams of his lost beloved's tears) and 'Der Doppelgänger' (where he shudders to see his own anguish imitated by his double). I wondered why he'd picked out those two: what was the story behind that? I wished Madame Lambert had told me about these translations before but, remembering what I'd just heard about her own loss, I could imagine why she hadn't.

When I left the night was calm and the sky clear, the stars extraordinarily bright as they often are down here. Driving home, I felt almost guilty because I seemed to understand Jean-Philippe so much better than his descendant – but it's easy to make the long dead less mysterious than the still living.

*

I don't see how you can ever reconcile yourself to losing the person you love most – genuinely accept it, I mean, really get over it; I couldn't. It must be worst for the happily married. Suppose, for instance, your wife or husband were knocked down and killed by a lorry just outside your house one day, before you'd even had time to say goodbye; how could you go on living there, or even in the same town? I know people do so because they've no choice, but how do they bear it? It's natural to want to die yourself if there's no one left to live for.

It's bad enough when he or she isn't actually dead, but only dead to you. Old-fashioned novelists used to say of bereaved or jilted characters that they 'found consolation in the arms of another', but how could a substitute truly console? Obviously, one could (literally) embrace an alternative, but it wouldn't be the same: that would be the point. It couldn't replace the one you'd lost, with that laugh, that walk, that way of saying hello, those eyes ('Stars, stars, and all eyes else dead coals,' as Leontes says), never to be restored.

*

An aphorism from one of Jean-Philippe's notebooks: 'Le réel, c'est lointain, ou dans le passé.' He's often sententious, and I think he was secretly vain of his line in world-weary maxims. Still, he gets it right now and then. Sometimes, when I'm working in the library, my present life becomes so spectral that it's as if I were a figment of my own imagination. When I'm sitting over my coffee in the restaurant I usually go to, trying to read my book (usually Shakespeare – I can't concentrate on novels at the moment), I'm quite surprised anyone notices me since to myself I seem almost invisible. I know it's illogical to say that living with you was real and that being without you isn't, but that's how it feels. What happens to me now – little enough in any case – isn't authentic in the way it used to be, when you were there to validate it. I'm not only living abroad – I'm exiled from myself.

For instance: one morning you got out of bed early, leaving me – as you thought – still asleep. You pulled on your T-shirt and jeans, went over to the washbasin and let some cold water dribble on to your hands, patted your face with your damp palms, crossed to the desk, and began to work. You must have woken up with some idea in your head which you didn't want to lose. I watched you covertly as you sat, writing and reading by turns, running your hand through your uncombed hair from time to time, occasionally letting out a long breath. Suddenly you turned round and caught me with my eyes open. For a moment I thought I'd irritated you, spying on you like that, but then your expression softened – perhaps because of the way I was looking at you – and without saying anything you came over, leaned over, and pressed your half-open mouth on mine. I loved you so much I almost wept. I knew then that not many things as real as that would ever happen to me again. All the same, there are times when I'd rather forget it, as I expect you've done already.

*

I seem to have made a friend down here, at last. She's one of the local schoolteachers. She'd heard about me – St Pierre is small enough for everyone to know what everyone else is up to, sooner or later – and asked me to talk to her class about life in England. The kids had lots of absurd questions (Why is it so foggy in London? Have you met the Princess of Wales?) but it did me good to be in the midst of all that energy, after spending so much time with the absent and the dead. Hélène is very well read in that daunting French way, and takes an interest in my work. I've begun to suspect that Laroche knew Berlioz, and she comes from the area round Grenoble, not far from where the composer was born. She feels a bit *depaysée*, so far from home. We talk partly in English, partly in French, so it's good practice for both of us.

I like Hélène's company, but it feels strange after being with you so much, although her self-possession and reserve make it easier. She hasn't volunteered anything about her private life and I don't ask, not wanting to provoke enquiries in return. The little formalities of French manners, even between familiar friends, reassure me – the handshake, firm but not prolonged, as one says *salut*, for instance. Hélène and I are still on a 'vous' basis. I feel too unsure of my ground to risk using 'tu', and she may feel that it's not for her to start doing so.

An example of her poise: we went to the cinema in the main town of the region, twenty kilometres away. It was the sort of French film that doesn't get shown much in England, unless late at night on television, excruciatingly dubbed into American. It was rubbish really, but had just enough style to be discussable and more than enough eroticism to be commercial. Sitting next to Hélène, I began to feel a little awkward as the camera grazed on the rich pasture of the heroine's body during a bedroom scene, until she turned towards me and half-whispered an ironic 'Oh, là-là' that defused the situation. At a tense moment later on she took my hand briefly, but I don't think it meant anything, and certainly it didn't lead to anything. Nor, of course, do I want it to.

*

I'm still so tired, much of the time, that like everyone else in St Pierre I go to bed fairly early, but last night I couldn't get to sleep for some reason. Despite my fatigue I felt too agitated to read, and I didn't like to listen to the radio so late for fear of disturbing the rest of the house. I got up, opened the shutters, and looked out. Clear sky, full moon, all quiet, except for a distant dog. I couldn't tell whether the moon had not long risen or was soon to set. Its low angle deepened the corrugations of the roof-tiles while draining them of colour, and created pockets of shadow not there during the day. I thought of Laroche, walking at night through the streets below, as he loved to do. And inevitably I thought of you, wondering if you were asleep, lying on your right side as usual with your left arm over your face, or whether you were still up, reading or talking late. I missed you so much I had to do something.

I dressed as fast as I could, let myself out gingerly so as not to wake the sleeping Charpentiers, and walked across the town to the river. The parked cars that I passed looked utterly inert, as if they would never move again. I made for the long *quai* by the bridge, where the locals fish and the tourists set out their picnic lunches. During the day you never hear the river, but because everything else was silent – even the dog had settled down – the chuckling sound of the water obstructed by the bridge's stone piers was as distinct as the tinkle made by the stream that fed into it on the far side. I stayed there listening and looking at the river's pearly sheen until the mists began to form, and I started to shiver.

I suppose I must have been calmer by the time I got back. At any rate I dropped off immediately. When Madame Charpentier knocked on the door with my coffee and said it was nearly nine, I could hardly believe it.

*

I keep hoping that one day I'll get a letter from you and reading between the lines I'll know you need me, something will have happened, and I'll set off there and then, travelling all day, through the night, across the channel, until I get to you, and you'll say it's good you're here, I didn't think you'd make it so soon, and I'll help you with whatever the problem is, we'll sort it out, we'll be

141

in touch again, I'll be part of your life again – but although that's what I hope for I'm afraid that it's not going to happen, that's not how things do happen, and your letter won't come.

*

The St Pierre *fête* happens very late in the year – I don't know why. It's always a gamble with the weather, Madame Charpentier tells me, but the evening turned out fine and dry. The *bal populaire* was indoors anyway, in the *foyer rural*. Hélène persuaded me to go, although I wasn't keen at first. It was rather chaotic, but touching at times. The music came partly from the latest disco to reach these remote regions, and partly from an accordion group out of a French film of the Thirties. Almost everyone danced, the teenagers (the girls especially) impassively anxious to show their sophistication, their grandparents joining them during the old favourites, smiling because they saw their own youth reflected in their partners' eyes. Hélène and I were about to take the floor ourselves, when a man about my age pushed me aside and insisted on dancing with her. She didn't look pleased, but no doubt wanted to avoid a scene. When they'd got to the other side of the hall they stopped, and after some apparently irritable words Hélène broke away; he too turned on his heel, and went out through the exit. 'C'est un ami, ce type?' I asked tentatively. 'Non, pas du tout,' she replied, in a tone which closed the subject.

There were only a few roundabouts and stalls outside, but enough noise and light to bring back the fairs of my childhood. I had a go at the rifle range because I wanted to win something to give Hélène, to cheer her up, but as usual failed to hit anything. She insisted on trying the dodgems and drove so aggressively that we soon caused several snarl-ups. When the other drivers began to shout at her, she threw up her arms, abandoned the car where it was in the middle of the mêlée, and walked off, leaving me to follow sheepishly in her wake. When we were not far from her house, she stopped under one of St Pierre's sporadic street-lamps, looked at my face under the light for a moment, and then said in English, 'I'm sorry if I was stupid. I hope I haven't spoiled your evening. Come in for a drink, and let's forget about it.' She took my arm until we reached the front door.

Her room was tidy, the books neatly shelved; no television. No armchairs either – Hélène doesn't seem to go in for comfort, or perhaps can't afford it. We had our coffee and cognac sitting at the central table, and talked for a long time, mostly about love. It was the sort of conversation you can't have in England without feeling embarrassed, or at least self-conscious, but in fact it was very academic and impersonal – *l'amour chez* Proust, Laclos, Stendhal – that sort of thing. I argued that being in love meant that you were closer to the real; Hélène said that it was simply 'le solipsisme à deux'. She must have her reasons for thinking that, just as I have mine for thinking otherwise.

I was so exhausted when I got home that I immediately lay down on the bed without undressing. I almost felt like crying out of sheer vexation; what was the use of talking about it? What I needed to know was how to bear it – the attrition, I mean – day after day, month by month, and nothing either of us had said helped me in the slightest.

*

There's something I've been meaning to tell you but somehow haven't liked to, perhaps because it feels vaguely disloyal. A few weeks ago I was sitting in the library as usual, trying to concentrate on the sorrows of Jean-Philippe without letting them remind me too much of my own, when I found I'd written down this sentence: 'Although he didn't know it at the time, it was the last day they were to spend together.' I looked at it with amazement, like Crusoe staring at the footprint in the sand. It gradually extended itself into a short story about a love affair between a young woman and a married man. It's the real thing for both of them, but he can't leave his wife, she finds someone else, he's devastated and thinks about suicide; by the end he's begun to hope that he'll get over it, although it's not clear that he will. I'm afraid it's all rather conventional. The true subject is closer to home, as you'll immediately realize. I'm sorry about that, but it's hardly surprising.

Since then I've written a few more brief tales in a similar vein. Perhaps I should try to make them hang together in some way, even though what they really have in common is what's behind them. Anyway, I keep this slightly shameful activity for the evenings, lest poor Laroche should be neglected. I tell myself that it's better than sitting around drinking too much, but I probably drink even more to cheer myself up, since my little narratives always end so disconsolately. It's not only the absence or loss of the other that keeps recurring, it's the death in the self, the death of the new life in the self created by love of the other, the real self you never knew about until being in love released it, the true self you found at last, only to lose it again.

You can see why these *contes tristes* don't actually help me much, and I may not go on with them after all. I wish you could look at them over my shoulder and tell me whether they're a waste of time or not – I'm sure you'd know – but if you were here to read them I wouldn't have invented them.

Sometimes I think I'd like to write about lovers being reunited – after being separated by the sea perhaps, as if returned from the dead, restored to each other on the far shore of despair – but that might only make matters worse.

*

While I was living above the café I often used to pass the church in the centre of St Pierre, and I still stop sometimes in my walks to look at the stone carvings round the door. They're romanesque, and its best feature, according to Michelin. I specially like a small, worn figure of Lazarus; he looks as if he's wondering whether his return to life is such a good move after all. Yesterday, feeling more than usually low, I went inside for the first time, but the interior is austere and there isn't much to see. I sat down all the same, and after a while leant forward with my face in my hands and my hands on the back of the chair in front. I suppose I must have looked as

144

if I were praying. I wish I could have done, in a way, but what would have been the point? I thought of all the prayers ascending at that moment all over France, like fountains whose water-drops rise only to fall back, and felt ashamed to bring my pitiful pain to such a place. After all, being unhappy in love is not like having cancer.

Out of the corner of my half-closed eye I saw the lower skirt of a hovering *soutane*, and got up abruptly. As I emerged through the wooden door into the street, the bright light made me blink. I went down to the bridge as I so often do, leaned over it, and studied the flow of the water. The river's surface was furrowed by a light breeze, making it difficult for a couple of anglers further along to keep track of their floats. They didn't seem to be having much luck, but looked philosophical.

*

Last night I did something stupid: I tried to ring you up. It simply hadn't occurred to me before, but I had to telephone my bank in England about transferring some money to the Crédit Agricole, and I suddenly realized how easy it now is to get through. Both the Charpentiers were out for the evening, and I had the place to myself, which is unusual. It was stupid because, for one thing, I can't be certain that you're still at the same number (except that my letters to you aren't returned marked 'Gone Away', as I dread they one day will be). I was so overcome, in the silent house, by my longing to hear your voice that I couldn't help myself. My hand shook so much I could hardly dial. I had no idea what I would say. I had to hang on for what seemed a long time before a man answered whose voice I didn't know. I hadn't bargained for this, and put the receiver down without saying anything. I couldn't very well ask him if he was your friend or not, and if so, what sort of friend. All sorts of possibilities occurred to me, naturally. I've no right to be jealous; perhaps I've no reason to be; in any case, it was absurd to panic. I've only myself to blame; I should have kept my distance. But we were so close – at least I thought we

were – that I don't know how to be separate any more. I've lost
my nerve.

*

My birthday last Friday. I kept saying to myself that I mustn't
expect a letter or even a card from you, but I hoped for one all
the same, so I was disappointed. I wish I knew whether you'd
remembered but decided not to do anything about it, or simply
forgot. Not that it makes much difference, since both alternatives
are equally painful.

I had a present from Hélène though – a copy of Berlioz's *Memoirs*
which she gave me because of its descriptions of her own *pays*. I've
read as far as the moment when the adolescent Hector, lying in
anguish on the ground, tears up handfuls of flowers and earth,
overcome by his sense of absence and isolation. I haven't quite
got to that stage yet myself, but one knows the feeling.

She also felt the occasion deserved a serious lunch. We went to
a restaurant in an old mill, newly restored, further up the river.
Six – or was it seven – courses appeared in inexorable succession;
it was Sunday after all. The atmosphere was decorous to start with
but became more and more carnivalesque, the tables littered with
gastronomic debris, the children running wild between them until
sent off by parents too bemused by food and drink to follow. We
didn't stagger outside ourselves before mid-afternoon.

We went down to the river through a deserted campsite, the leaves
now falling where the tents had been. On this side there were trees to
the water's edge; on the other a grey cliff loomed high above them,
and us. I tried to teach Hélène how to make stones skip on the
water's surface, but time hadn't made them smooth enough, and
I had to give up. She asked me what I planned to do when I got
back to England, and whether I was homesick. Were there any
friends I particularly missed? She'd never probed in this way
before. I didn't know what to say – in fact, I felt too upset to
say anything, and just shrugged. 'Ah,' she said understandingly,
'c'est comme ça.' 'Effectivement, c'est comme ça – c'est toute une

146

histoire.' But as I tried to find the right words to continue she put her finger across my mouth, to shut me up. 'Pas d'histoires,' she said, 'il vaut mieux, non?' I was glad she stopped me: how could I have begun to explain it all? 'Tu es très sympa, Hélène,' I said.

We walked for some time along the bank, peering into the water now and then, trying to see the fish, but it was already too deep and brown with the autumn rain, and winter coming on. We held hands as we went back to the car, and kissed each other on the cheek when we parted.

I don't quite know what to do. I can't tell her outright that I'm not available without appearing to assume that she's interested − and I've no idea if that's the case because, although I like being with her, I can't read her. You see how difficult you make things for me, even now. Still, it's not your fault, I know.

*

When I sit writing in the evenings in the dim light of the table-lamp, *un coup de rouge* to hand, I often have the radio on, although the sound quality isn't good. It's too lonely otherwise. I usually listen to *France Musique*, but I'm always apprehensive lest they should play something we've heard together; yesterday it finally happened. After patronizingly introducing Elgar as an obscure eccentric, a sort of English Magnard, the announcer put on a not very good recording of the *Enigma Variations*. I naturally thought of the concert we went to last summer, during the festival. I saw you so clearly in my head, sitting next to me in the crowded hall, listening intently as you always do, so rapt. I wondered what was going through your mind, but you wouldn't say. It excited me that the work should mean so much to you, but it also hurt me that, because of it, I couldn't reach you.

All the same, I was glad to hear the music again because I realize better now what the enigma is − how you have to hide your true subject in order to express it, so that there's always something too recessed to be got at, but without which the work wouldn't exist. I know it's not a great new thought, but it struck me freshly, as I sat there, trying in my feeble way to live with what was real by making variations on it which were not. Even if you had told me what you were thinking about, it would have been a story of some kind, to keep me quiet.

And yet I shouldn't like you to think that what I write to you isn't true – it's absolutely true, as far as it goes. The only reason it doesn't go further is that I don't want to annoy you by going on and on. If I told you how it really is without you, hour by hour, you'd think I was making it up.

*

A discovery: my hunch about Laroche and Berlioz was right. A couple of days ago I found an excited letter from Laroche to his sister which proves that he was in the audience at the first performance in December 1830 of the *Symphonie Fantastique*. He sat just behind the enthusiastic Liszt, and Jean-Philippe himself was obviously knocked out by both the event and the work. This must be why, later on, he asked Berlioz to set a cycle of his poems. He may have heard rumours of the composer's passion for the then inaccessible actress Harriet Smithson, and thought that Berlioz might sympathize with his own longings. Nothing seems to have come of the idea, but I ought to check whether there are any relevant papers in the Berlioz museum. I could go over there with Hélène, when she returns home for Christmas.

I've also turned up a draft of an unfinished poem called 'Le Retour'. Its sentiments are predictable – the poet wants to go back to his native country and the woman he loves but fears she'll send him away again – but they ring true to me. It's entirely possible that when Laroche went to Paris as a *jeune homme de province* (like a character in Balzac), he left behind in St Pierre someone he missed more than he'd expected to. I wonder who she was, and whether she did reject him. Perhaps she had been attracted but was persuaded that marriage would be too much of a risk: Jean-Philippe sometimes sounds off-puttingly self-centred, although that may partly be the effect of the conventions in which he wrote.

I'm aware, of course, that I'm in danger of identifying with him because by the image of my cause I see the portraiture of his, as Hamlet puts it. But if 'Le Retour' was merely a routine Romantic exercise, why does it break off abruptly in mid-line, as if the emotion the poet was trying to express had become too much for him, and why is the handwriting (which I now know so well) so much more agitated than usual?

*

I was walking along the Embankment. It must have been about this time of year, and getting dark. The crowds of people going home from work thickened continually. The pavement was uneven – it was being relaid – so I kept my eyes on the ground, watching my step. Someone jostled me off-balance and I had to step aside, into the gutter. I looked up, and there you were, under the next street-lamp. I felt so breathless, as if I'd been running flat out for a long time, that I couldn't move. You went on walking towards me with that slight sway which I love so much, but with a slowed motion, almost floating, as if you were on film. You wondered whether to pass me by, but when you were near enough you said hello after all, in your usual way. In my agitation, still standing in the gutter, I clasped and unclasped my hands, although I know it's a habit which irritates you. Your smile faded, your eyes seemed to glisten, and you began to frown, as you do when you can't make something out. I wanted to explain, to take your hand, even to smooth with my fingers the faint line on your brow, but my mouth was so dry, like paper, that I still couldn't speak. I must have grimaced, in my distress.

When you were about forty yards further on my paralysis suddenly left me. Tripping over the kerb, I almost knocked down an old lady with a heavy bag. But the harder I struggled to catch you up, the more other people got in the way. Your figure diminished, as it receded. My legs got heavier and heavier, as I tried to force them against the tide. You turned on to the bridge. The streets on the other side were like dark tunnels, the houses in them shut up, the parked cars abandoned. There was no sign of you, nor of anybody

149

else. My fear that I'd lost you for good was now so great I had to cry out at last, and I began to shout 'Come back, come back, come back' at the top of my voice. As I woke, the echoes sounded loud enough to have roused the whole house, but Madame Charpentier didn't say anything, in the morning.

I rang Madame Lambert to say I couldn't come to the Maison because I wasn't well, and I've been out walking in the woods most of the day, trying to calm down. I know it doesn't seem much as I describe it, but I've never been so frightened by a dream in my life, and I've got to tell you about it so that you can stop it coming true. Promise me you won't ever walk away like that.

Fortunately I've got some sleeping tablets left over. I'll make sure to take one tonight, if not two.

*

You'll be surprised to get a letter on this hotel – or rather motel – notepaper. I felt so exhausted after driving for so long that I took the first place I could find. It's just off the motorway and on the edge of a *zone industrielle*. There can't be much of an outlook in the daytime – or of an inlook at any time. The walls are pale; on them hang two landscapes so anonymous as to be almost invisible; there is a bed and a chair, and a laminated worktop with a television on it at one end. I'm sitting at the other end writing because there's nothing to watch except a dubbed American *policier*, close-ups of wildlife, and an interminable interview with an author I've not heard of about a book I'll never read.

I decided to come back the day before yesterday. I didn't go to the Maison because it was Sunday. The weather was amazing, for so late in the year; it made me think how happy I should be, living in this climate, if I was happy to start with, as I'd hoped. The sun was warm at midday as it never is in England, after the leaves have fallen. I drove inland for a couple of hours, more or less at random, and found myself in a narrow wooded gorge. I left the car, climbed up to where the trees began to thin out, and sat down on a ledge to have my picnic. The rock behind my back was dry and grey, rough to the touch. A bird I couldn't spot kept calling at intervals from one tree and then another – a woodpecker, perhaps. On the other side of the defile the crest of the rock stood out sharply against the blue, the way it does in the light of the south. I couldn't see any buildings; nobody went along the road; the place seemed deserted. Looking down more carefully at the ground near me, I saw a flattish stone I'd missed before. On its face was the crisp print of a little shell, its ridges spreading out like a tiny fan half open.

I cut my *baguette* open longways, filled it with cheese, and had eaten about half of it when a bit of crust stuck in my throat. I tried to wash it down with some wine, but it went the wrong way. Even after I'd finally dislodged it I still felt as if I was choking. All this made my eyes water and, once started, I began to sob as I've never done before, not since childhood anyway. It was as if breathing and crying were the same thing, as if tears were all that life came to. For the first time I consciously wanted to die. I'm not sure how long this lasted – I didn't think to look at my watch – but as it subsided I knew I couldn't go on, not so far away, so cut off, so out of touch, not any more. When I came abroad I thought it might help me because there was no way I'd see you or hear about you, but now I couldn't bear it any longer, for the same reason.

Eventually I made myself finish off the bread and wine so as to have enough strength to get back. The sun had begun to lose its unseasonal warmth. As I slowly returned along the river valley to St Pierre I planned my get-out. I explained it all to you, in the car, as I drove. It was such a relief to talk, at last.

It's easy to take drastic action once you put your mind to it. I realized that, since my arrival, I'd been living for my departure. I told Madame Charpentier that I had to go home suddenly for family reasons, and wrote apologetic notes to Madame Lambert and, of course, to Hélène. I felt bad about leaving them so abruptly, but it couldn't be helped. I bundled my clothes, books and notes into my suitcases, put them in the car, and here I am, in this characterless cell in the middle of nowhere, but on my way.

I'll post this as soon as I get back to England, to our city, where there'll always be a chance I'll run into you, sooner or later, or see you in the distance, where I can at least haunt the streets you tread, that we trod, before you left, before I left.

*

The night ferry was strangely empty, due to the time of year I suppose. The few passengers immediately made for their cabins, leaving the bars quiet; the restaurant was closed anyway. I'd decided I'd got to catch this boat because I couldn't face another night in France, and so I'd been driving hard all day; I sat up for a while all the same, and had a drink or two. I glanced at an English newspaper lying on the table, but couldn't concentrate – in fact, I could barely understand it. I felt I'd been on another planet.

When I finally lay down it took me ages to drop off, and I did so only to wake again, so that I hardly knew whether I was conscious or not. The sea was extraordinarily calm, the ship floating forward smoothly, almost by stealth, its usual vibrations barely noticeable. I must have dreamed at least once because I had the distinct impression that I wasn't on my bunk but in a coffin, newly made and still open. The cabin ceiling, with its air-conditioning grille, was so unlike any conceivable kind of tomb that I wondered if I was in some sort of mortuary, waiting for the hearse perhaps. After this I gave up trying to sleep, and went on deck. Dense fog on all sides. As I waited for it to clear, it occurred to me that the source of my nightmare might have been Laroche's poem 'Au Cimitière', in which he petulantly tells his beloved that if she isn't more sympathetic he'll soon be in his grave, and then she'll be sorry. Jean-Philippe's occasional attempts at Gothic *frisson* don't carry much conviction.

Out in the air it wasn't as cold as I expected; the fog seemed to blanket the wind. Now and then the boat sounded its horn, and was echoed by muffled replies from invisible companions. Then the vapour began to thin, and through its wraiths gleamed three sharply pointed white rocks, followed by a wall of blanched cliff. The moonlight caught the froth of the waves at their feet. A few moments later the fog came down again and didn't lift until I made out the sprinkled lights of the docks. Behind them orderly lines of street-lamps, leading away into the interior, gradually faded as the grey dawn took over.

*

Before I left St Pierre I'd rung Tom, to ask if I could stay for a couple of days. He said he was about to go away himself, but I was welcome to keep the flat warm. On no account, however, was I to touch the word processor. It's the only thing that's changed since I was last here. It dominates the usual clutter of books and papers on his desk, but its clouded screen gives nothing away. I was surprised to see it since Tom had always resisted getting one so strongly. It takes over what you feel, he used to say, detaches you from what you write, makes it too alien, too other; it had a style, and probably a life, of its own. Perhaps that was why, in the end, he'd been converted to it.

I didn't dare go over to the window when I arrived, but lay down on the sofa and immediately went to sleep. Driving on the other side of the road again must have tired me out. When I woke it was dark once more, and at first I couldn't think where I was. I studied the way light from the street spread across the ceiling. I didn't feel hungry, although I'd eaten almost nothing since I'd left France.

I thought of how often I'd called here, hoping to catch sight of you as you returned to your room, so like this one, in the house opposite. I remembered the one time I was lucky – when you came into view at last, stopped to find your key, and closed the front door behind you. I could feel my heart beat while I waited for you to reappear at your window. You opened it to let in the air, because of the heat. Turning away, you pulled off your T-shirt over your head, your white back sinking into the room's depths. I remembered too how many times I'd walked along this street, hoping I'd meet you, how many other streets I'd walked along, hoping to glimpse you, before you were there whenever I wanted you, in our flat on the other side of the city. I decided that tomorrow, or the next day, I'd go round and find out whether my letters had arrived, and if they'd been sent on, to wherever you are now.

But what if, after all, you'd come back to where you used to be, to the old room over the way? Why hadn't I thought of that before? You were always fond of it. You hadn't really wanted to move.

*

As I stand up, I have to steady myself by holding on to the arm of the sofa, until the dizziness ceases. I walk carefully past the desk, through the shadows, towards the window. I rest my forehead against the pane and look across, but nothing moves beyond the untroubled glass. I look down, and on the pavement below an abject figure waits under the light. As he gazes upwards, he wrings his hands. I can see his features as clearly as if I were looking in a mirror.